A Garland Series

The
Flowering of the Novel

Representative Mid-Eighteenth
Century Fiction
1740-1775

A Collection of 121 Titles

The Siege of Calais

Claudine Tencin

Garland Publishing, Inc., New York & London

1974

———————

Bibliographical note:

this facsimile has been made from a copy in the
Yale University Library
(Hfd29.223m)

———————

Library of Congress Cataloging in Publication Data

Tencin, Claudine Alexandrine Guérin de, 1682-1749.
  The siege of Calais.

  (The Flowering of the novel)
  Ascribed to C. A. G. de Tencin and A. de Ferriol,
comte d'Pont de Veyle. Cf. Barbier, A.-A. Dict. des
ouvrages anonymes.
  Reprint of the 1740 ed. printed for T. Woodward,
London.
    I. Pont de Veyle, Antoine de Ferriol, comte d',
1700-1788, joint author. II. Title. III. Series.
PZ3.T2532Si5 [PQ2067.T2] 843'.5 74-16066
ISBN 0-8240-1101-5

Printed in the United States of America

THE

SIEGE of *CALAIS*

BY

EDWARD of ENGLAND.

An HISTORICAL NOVEL.

Tranflated from the FRENCH Original.

LONDON,

Printed for T. WOODWARD, at the *Half-Moon* between the *Temple-Gates* in *Fleet-ftreet*; and PAUL VAILLANT, againft *Southampton-Street* in the *Strand.*
MDCCXL.

ADVERTISEMENT.

THIS Piece is esteem'd for its Politeness equal to the *Princess of Cleves*, and according to the Report of a certain Great Lady, (not long since arriv'd from *Paris*, and lately, on her Lord's Death, return'd thither again) is at present the most in Vogue of any Book of the Kind, not only at the *French* Court, but among all the *Beau Monde* at *Paris* and elsewhere in that Kingdom.

lifts. The Weather. Hope. Education. Prating.
Modern Inventions. Luxury. Libels. Popular
Difcontents. Great Men. Theatrical Entertainments. Method in Writing. Suicide. Infidelity.
Publick Sports. Levity. The Duty of Authors.
A Club of Authors. Happinefs. Women. Coffee-Houfes. Mafquerades. Patriotifm. Bifhop Burnet's Hiftory. Mortality. The Character of different Nations. Sedition Hopers. Some Characters of the prefent Age. Vol. II. The fecond Edition.

IV. The Life and ftrange furprifing Adventures
of *Robinfon Crufoe* of *York*, Mariner; who lived
eight and twenty Years all alone in an uninhabited
Ifland on the Coaft of *America*, near the Mouth of
the great River *Oronoque*, having been caft on
Shore by Shipwreck, wherein all the Men perifhed
but himfelf. With an Account how he was at laft
as ftrangely delivered by Pyrates. Written by himfelf. The Eighth Edition, adorn'd with Cuts. In
two Volumes.

V. Pope's and Swift's Mifcellanies, in 6 Volumes.

VI. A general Hiftory of the Pyrates from their
firft Rife and Settlement in the Ifland of *Providence*,
to the prefent time. With the remarkable Actions
and Adventures of the two female Pyrates *Mary
Read*, and *Anne Bonny*; contain'd in the following
Chapters. Introduction, Chap. I. of Capt. *Avery*.
2. Of Capt. *Martel*. 3. Of Capt. *Teach*. 4. Of
Capt. *Bonnet*. 5. Of Capt. *England*. 6. Of Capt.
Vane. 7. Of Capt. *Rackham*. 8. Of Capt. *Davis*.
9. Of Capt. *Roberts*. 10. Of Capt. *Anftis*. 11. Of
Capt. *Worley*. 12. Of Capt. *Lowther* 13. Of
Capt. *Low*. 14. Of Capt. *Evans*. 15. Of Capt.
Phillips. 16. Of Capt. *Spriggs*. 17. Of Capt. *Smith*.
And their feveral Crews. To which is added a
fhort Abftract of the Statute and Civil Law, in relation

lation to Pyracy. In two Volumes. The fourth Edition. Vol. I. By Captain *Charles Johnson*.

VII. The History of the Pyrates; containing the Lives of Capt. *Misson*, Capt. *Bowen*, Capt. *Kidd*, Capt. *Tew*, Capt. *Halsey*, Capt. *White*, Capt. *Condent*, Capt. *Bellamy*, Capt. *Fly*, Capt. *Howard*, Capt. *Lewis*, Capt. *Cornelius*, Capt. *Williams*, Capt. *Burgess*, Capt. *North*; and their several Crews. Intermixed with a Description of *Magadoxa* in *Æthiopia*; the natural Hatred and Cruelty of the Inhabitants to all *Whites*; their Laws, Manners, Customs, Government and Religion: With a particular Account of the beautiful Tombs, and their Ceremony of guarding them, taken from Captain *Beavis*'s Journal; and that of a *Molotto*, who belong'd to the said Captain, was taken by and lived several Years with the *Magadoxians*. To the whole is added an Appendix, which compleats the Lives of the first Volume, corrects some Mistakes, and contains the Tryal and Execution of the Pyrates at *Providence*, under Governor *Rogers*; with some other necessary Insertions, which did not come to hand till after the Publication of the first Volume, and which makes up what was defective: Collected from Journals of Pyrates, brought away by a Person who was taken by, and forced to live with them twelve Years; and from those of Commanders, who had fallen into their hands, some of whom have permitted their Names to be made use of, as a Proof of the Veracity of what we have published: The whole instructive and entertaining. Vol. II. By the Author of Vol. I.

VIII. The Royal Dictionary abridged; in two Parts. 1. *French* and *English*. 2. *English* and *French*. Containing above five Thousand Words more than any *French* and *English* Dictionary yet extant. And to which are added the Accents of all *English* Words, to facilitate their Pronunciation to Forreigners.

The

The Sixth Edition, carefully corrected. As also an Alphabetical List of the most common Christian Names of Men and Women, and the Abbreviations of the said Names vulgarly used. By Mr. *A. Boyer*.

IX. The History of the Conquest of *Mexico* by the *Spaniards*. Translated into *English* from the original *Spanish* of Don *Antonio de Solis*, Secretary and Historiographer to his Catholick Majesty. By *Tho. Townsend* Esq; late Lieutenant Collonel in Brigadier *Newton*'s Regiment. The whole Translation revised and corrected by *Nathanael Hooke* Esq; Translator of *The Travels of* Cyrus, *and the Life of the Archbishop of* Cambray.

X. The History of Queen *Anne*. Wherein all the Civil and Military Transactions of that memorable Reign are faithfully compiled from the best Authorities, and Impartially related. The whole intermixed with several authentick and remarkable Papers. Together with all the important Debates in Parliament; a compleat List of the most eminent Persons who died in the Course of this Reign, with proper Characters of those who rendered themselves most conspicuous in Church and State. Illustrated with a regular Series of all the Medals that were struck to commemorate the great Events of this Reign: With a Variety of other useful and ornamental Plates. By Mr. *A. Boyer*.

XI. Memoirs of the Duke *de Villars*, Marshal General of the Armies of his Most Christian Majesty. Containing his Rise under the most famous *French* Generals of the last Age; the Difficulties he met with from the Ministry; his Intrigues at the Court of *Bavaria*; and his secret Negociations in *Vienna*, relating to the Succession of the *Spanish* Monarchy. Intermixed with a great Number of Military Observations on the Battles in which he fought: Extracted from original Papers. Translated from the *French*.

XII. The

XII. The History of the Revolutions of *Poland,* from the Foundation that Monarchy to the Death of *Augustus* II. Br. Mr. *l'Abbé des Fontaines*. Translated from the *French*.

XIII. A Collection of several Tracts of the Right Honourable *Edward* Earl of *Clarendon,* Author of *The History of the Rebellion,* and *Civil Wars of* Flanders. *Viz.* I. A Discourse, by Way of Vindication of himself from the Charge of High Treason brought against him by the House of Commons. II. Reflections upon several Christian Duties, Divine and Moral, by Way of Essays. 1. Human Nature. 2. Of Life. 3. Reflections upon the Happiness which we enjoy in and from ourselves. 4. Of impudent Delight in Wickedness. 5. Of Drunkenness. 6. Of Envy. 7. Of Pride. 8. Of Anger. 9. Of Patience in Adversity. 10. Of Contempt of Death, and the best providing for it. 11. Of Friendship. 12. Of Council and Conversation. 13. Of Promises. 14. Of Liberty. 15. Of Industry. 16. Of Sickness. 17. Of Repentance. 18. Of Conscience. 19. Of an Active and Contemplative Life, and when and why the one ought to be preferred to the other. 20. Of War. 21. Of Peace. 22. Of Sacrilege. 23. A Discourse of the Reverence due to Antiquity. 24. A Discourse against multiplying Controversies. by insisting upon Particulars not necessary to the Point in Debate. 25. A Dialogue concerning the Want of Respect due to Age. 26. A Dialogue concerning Education, *&c.* 28. Contemplations and Reflections upon the Psalms of *David,* with Devotions suitable to the Trouble of the Times.

N. B. None of these Pieces were ever printed before; and the Original Manuscript, in his Lordship's Hand-writing, may be seen at *T. Woodward's.*

BOOKS printed for and sold by PAUL VAILLANT *over-against* Southampton-Street *in the* Strand.

I. Nouvelle Histoire d'Angleterre en Francois et en Anglois; or, a New History of England in French and English by Question and Answer, extracted from the most celebrated English Historians, particularly M. de Rapin Thoyras 12mo.

N. B. This Work was calculated for two Purposes, First instructing Youth in the History of their Country, which ought to be their first Study, and much preferable to their learning the Histories of ancient Empires and Kingdoms, Secondly, facilitating at the same time their learning the French Tongue.

II. Novelas Examplares de Miguel de Cervantes Saavedra dirigidas à la Excelentissima Señora Condessa de Westmorland, en esta ultima Imprecion corrigidas por Pedro Pineda, y adornadas de muy bellas Estampas, 2 Vol. 12mo.

III. Typi Declinationum & Conjugationum Nominum & Verborum Linguæ Græcæ, in Usum Scholarum.

IV. Græcæ

Books printed for PAUL VAILLANT.

IV. Græcæ Linguæ Dialecti in Scholæ Regiæ Weftmonafterienfis Ufum Recognitæ. Opera Mich. Maittaire. Præfationem & Appendicem ex Apollonii Dyfcoli Fragmento Inedito addidit J. F. Reitzius. 8ᵛᵒ.

V. M. Manilii Aftronomicon ex Recenfione & cum Notis R. Bentleii. *Charta Majori & Minori.* 4ᵗᵒ.

VI. Reflexions politiques fur les Finances & le Commerce ou l'on Examine quelles ont été fur les Revenus les Denrées, le Change étranger, & Confequemment fur notre Commerce, les Influences des Augmentations & des Diminutions des Valeurs numeraires des Monnoyes, par Mr. *Du Totte,* 2 Vol. 12*mo.*

VII. Recueil des Pieces de Poefie de Mr. *de Voltaire,* avec fon Effay, fur l'Hiftoire du Siecle *de Louis* XIV. 8*vo.*

VIII. A new Dictionary Spanifh and Englifh, and Englifh and Spanifh; containing the Etymology, the proper and metaphorical Signification of Words, Terms of Art and Sciences, Names of Men, Families, Places, and of the principal Plants in *Spain* and the *Weft-Indies,* together with the Arabick and Moorifh Words, now commonly received in the Spanifh Tongue, An Explanation of the difficult Words, Proverbs and Phrafes in *Don Quixote* and other the moft celebrated Writers in that Language; correcting the Errors, and fupplying the Defects in other Dictionaries, by the Addition
of

E R R A T A.

Page 6. Line 10. *from* read *for.* P. 33. l. 6.
left r. *laft.* P. 81. l. 5. *Mademoifelle's* r. *Mademoifelle de Mailly's.* P. 115. laft line *Deliverers*
r. *Deliverer.* P. 119. l. 16. *fhe* r. *be.* P. 128.
l. 4. *Ting* r. *Thing.*

THE
SIEGE of *CALAIS*,

BY

EDWARD of ENGLAND.

PART I.

MONSIEUR *de Vienne* *, defcended from one of the moft confiderable Families in *Burgundy*, had only one Daughter by his Marriage with Mademoifelle *de Chauvirey*.

THE Birth, the Fortune, and, above all, the Beauty of Mademoifelle *de Vienne*

---

* M. *de Vienne* was Governor of *Calais* when *Edward* III. befieged it, in the Year 1347. See Morery.

B   excited

excited the Love and Courtſhip of as
many as could pretend to the Honour of
an Alliance with Mr. *de Vienne*. Mr. *de
Granſon*, who was equally well deſcended,
had the Preference over all his Rivals.
He was both amiable and amorous, and
yet did not touch the Heart of Mademoiſelle *de Vienne* ; but *Virtue* ſupplied
the Place of *Senſibility*. She diſcharged
her Duty in ſo natural and eaſy a Manner, that Mr. *de Granſon* might well
enough ſuppoſe he was beloved : But he
was not long pleaſed with a Happineſs
which ceaſed to coſt him Trouble.

H E had ſcarce been married a Year,
before he looked out for Pleaſures leſs
calm, ariſing from new Amuſements.
Madam *de Granſon* beheld her Huſband's
Coldneſs with a ſort of Pain ; the Concerns of Beauty being almoſt as dear to a
young Lady as thoſe of her Heart.

S H E had, from her earlieſt Years,
been united in a tender Friendſhip with
the

the Counteſs *de Beaumont*, Siſter to Mr. *de Canaple.* One Day, when there had been a great deal of Company at Madam *de Granſon*'s, and Madam *de Beaumont* had perceived ſhe did not join in Converſation with that Freedom ſhe uſed to do; I have a great Mind, ſaid Madam *de Beaumont* to her, as ſoon as they were alone, to gueſs at what makes you ſo thoughtful. Do not offer to gueſs at it, I beg you, anſwered Madam *de Granſon*; let me hide from you a Weakneſs I am aſhamed of. You are in the wrong to be ſo, replied Madam *de Beaumont*; your Sentiments are not unreaſonable: Mr. *de Granſon* has done every thing that was neceſſary to make you love him; and now he does every thing that can tend to make you jealous of him. I aſſure you, ſaid Madam *de Granſon*, if I loved my Huſband in the manner you think I do, I ſhould not be aſhamed of being concerned at his preſent Behaviour; but I never loved him beyond what my Duty obliged me to: *His* Heart is by no means

eſſential

effential to the Happinefs of *Mine* ; but it provokes me, that the few Attractives, whatever they may be, which I am Miftrefs of, fhould be overlooked and defpifed. It mortifies me, that a Year's Marriage fhould have extinguifhed my Hufband's Paffion ; and I am vexed at myfelf, for feeling fuch Emotions as are only excufable when they are occafioned by Love.

Your good Brother, who has never feen me, continued fhe, but who was the Confident of Mr. *de Granfon*'s Paffion, and to whom, when we were firft married, he may poffibly have boafted of his Happinefs, will wonder to find him, at his Return, in love with another Woman. He ought indeed to wonder at it, faid Madam *de Beaumont* ; but I can affure you he will not. He thinks it impoffible for a Man to be long enamoured and happy ; but withal, he is far from thinking, as moft of his Sex do, that a Man can be falfe to a Woman,

without

without forfeiting his Honour : He is, on the contrary, perfuaded, that a Man cannot be too virtuous an Obferver of an Engagement, which oftentimes difor-ders the whole Life of an unhappy Wo-man, who has been made to believe fhe fhould always be beloved : And there-fore, added Madam *de Beaumont*, my Brother has never indulged himfelf in a ferious Engagement.

I A M forry to hear you talk thus, an-fwered Madam *de Granfon* ; the Intimacy which is between Mr. *de Canaple* and Mr. *de Granfon*, and that which is be-tween us two, had raifed in me a Hope to make him my Friend ; but I am afraid he would prove as inconftant in Friend-fhip as in Love. It is not the fame Thing, replied Madam *de Beaumont* : Friendfhip has not, like Love, one de-termined Object ; and it is this Object, once gained, which fpoils All with my Brother. But I much queftion, whether he would be over-hafty to be one of Your

Friends: He is afraid of seeing women he might love; and you are formed in such a manner, as may very justly make him afraid. I cannot help thinking too, that though he is a very amiable Man, he will not at all appear so to you: For I must let you into this farther small Particular of his Character; his *Wit* never shews itself to better Advantage, than when he has nothing to fear from his *Heart*. That is to say, replied Madam *de Granson*, he is shocking every time he seeks to please; and that he ought to be hated for it. In truth, you have a very singular Brother; and if you were like him, I should not love you so much as I do.

WHEN Madam *de Granson* was alone, she could not forbear revolving in her Mind the several Particulars she had just been hearing of Mr. *de Canaple's* Character. And so he fancies, says she, that, in order to be beloved, he need only to love. Ah! how well could I

convince

convince him of the contrary! and what a Pleasure would it be to me to mortify his Vanity! This Thought, which Madam *de Granson* found no Harm in, employed her more than it deserved. She enquired, with some sort of Impatience, of the Time when Mr. *de Canaple* was to come.

THAT Time was not far off. Mr. *de Granson* told his Wife, his Friend was upon the Road, and desired her Consent, that they might be lodged together, as they had always been. Some short time after this, he presented Mr. *de Canaple* to her: Few Men were so handsome as he; his whole Person was extremely graceful; but in his Aspect were such peculiar Charms, that it was next to impossible not to be taken with them.

MADAM *de Granson*, though prepossessed with his Character, could not forbear seeing him really as he was.

B 4.   As

As for him, his Eyes *only* found her beautiful; and in this Situation, being in no Fear for his Repose, he put no Restraint upon the Talent which he naturally had to please. Attentive, assiduous, observant, obliging, he saw Madam *de Granson* at all Hours, and always shone with new Graces. They had their Effect. Madam *de Granson* was some time without perceiving it: She sincerely believed, that the Design which she had to please him, was only a Desire to mortify his Vanity; but her Vexation at not succeeding therein, opened her Eyes, and gave her a true Notion of what she felt. Is it possible, said she, that I should owe all the Count *de Canaple*'s Obsequiousness, all his Complaisance, to nothing but his Indifference! But why should I go about to make myself be beloved by him? Who will warrant me, that I should prove insensible? Alas! the Resentment which his Indifference fills me with, does it not too plainly tell me

me how weak I am ? Inſtead of
ſtudying to pleaſe him, I muſt, on the
contrary, avoid ſeeing him. I am at
my Wits End, that I cannot make an
Impreſſion upon him ; and what ſhould
I be, if he inſpired me with Sentiments which I ought to reproach myſelf for ?

THIS Scheme of ſhunning Mr. *de
Canaple* was none of the eaſieſt to execute. Mr. *de Granſon*'s Houſe was become his : She herſelf had conſented to
it. What would the Publick think,
ſhould ſhe alter her Mind ? But, that
which ſhe feared much more, what
would Mr. *de Canaple* think ? Might
he not happen to ſuſpect the Truth ?

IT was a difficult Thing for her to
preſerve, amidſt ſo much Agitation,
the full Freedom of her Spirit. She
grew melancholy and mindleſs with
every body; and odd-humoured, and
almoſt capricious with Mr. *de Canaple:*

Some-

Sometimes, over-ruled by her Inclination, she paid him a pleasing Distinction; but as soon as ever she perceived it, she punished him for it by treating him quite ill. He was amazed, and even afflicted at what he looked upon as an Unevenness of Temper in Madam *de Granson*. He had observed in her so great a Share of Merit, that, without conceiving a Passion for her, he had at least conceived a great Esteem and a great Friendship for her.

MEAN while, the more he pleased, the more her ill Usage was increased. He was afraid at last that he had displeased; and spake of it to his Sister. I am fully persuaded, said Madam *de Beaumont* to him, that Madam *de Granson* loves her Husband more than she imagines. She is jealous; and perhaps suspects you have a Hand in the Gallantries by which she is injured. This is what sets her against you. She wrongs me, replied Mr. *de Canaple*; but

but that shall not make me take the less Pains for her Repose. I will employ my utmost Interest with her Husband to reclaim him. In good truth, said Madam *de Beaumont*, smiling, a Man who believes that the Alertness of Love ends where its Happiness begins, seems to me no very fit Preacher of Fidelity to a Husband.

BE my Way of Thinking what it will, replied Mr. *de Canaple*, it is certain, at least, that I could never find in my heart to make a Woman unhappy by whom I was beloved, and to whom I had given a Right to depend upon my Tenderness.

ALL this while Madam *de Granson* was continually obliged to see Mr. *de Canaple*; and not being able to overcome her Inclination towards him, she resolved to spend Part of the Summer at *Vermanton*, a Seat of her Husband's. Mr. *de Granson*, whose Wife's Presence

B 6   put

put him under some Restraints, readily consented to what she desired. But he left her not long in her Solitude. He fell out soon after with his Mistress; and Mr. *de Canaple* took hold of this Opportunity, and so powerfully represented to him the Duties he owed to his Wife, that he prevailed on him to go home to her again.

SOME Effect had been wrought on her by Mr. *de Canaple*'s Absence, together with the Reproaches she continually made to herself, for having, in despite of her Duty, been susceptible of an Inclination towards a Man, whose Indifference likewise had left her no Excuse for her Weakness. Mr. *de Granson* thought her Beauties improved, and renewed his Love to her with as much Ardour as ever. She received her Husband's Fondness with more Complacency than she had yet done. She thought she owed him this Compensation; and that she could not do too much to re-

pair

pair the secret Injury she was conscious
of doing him.

So long as she had been alone, she
avoided, under this Pretext, the seeing
any Company. Mr. *de Granson*'s Presence put an End to that, and brought
to his House, all the People of Distinction round about; among whom Mr.
de Canaple likewise came, at his Friend's
Solicitation. Madam *de Granson*, who
had promis'd herself to make no Distinction of him from the rest, either by
good or bad Treatment, gave him a
handsome Reception, and liv'd with
him in a very polite Manner. He ascribed this Alteration to the Counsel he
had given, and was thereby confirm'd
in the Opinion he had already enter-
tained of Madam *de Granson*'s Passion
for her Husband.

Mr. *de Granson* lov'd Pleasure; his
Wife, attentive to please him, fell in
with all the Amusements which the Country

try can afford. There was Hunting,
there was Fishing. and, oftentimes,
Dancing all Night long. The Count
de Canaple, in all these different Exer-
cises, shew'd a peculiar Gracefulness and
Address. As he had no particular Attachment, he gallanted all the Women,
he pleas'd them all ; and among all those
who were at Madam *de Granson*'s, there
was more than One with whom he might
have succeeded, had he had a Mind to
it ; but he was very far from desiring any
such Thing.

MR. *de Chalons*, whose Estate lay not
far off, was one of the earliest to visit
Monsieur and Madam *de Granson* ; he had
learn'd the first Rudiments of War in
company with the Count *de Canaple*.
They saw one another again with Pleasure,
and renew'd a Friendship which had begun during their youngest Years. Mr.
de Chalons invited the Count *de Canaple*
to come and pass some Time with him,
at a Seat he had within a League of
Vermanton.

Vermanton; Hunting was their principal
Occupation. The Count *de Canaple*,
being hotly engaged in the Purſuit of a
Stag, found himſelf alone, at the Beginning of the Night, in the Midſt of
the Foreſt. Being acquainted with all
the Routs of it, and finding himſelf not
far off of *Vermanton*, he directed his
Courſe thither. It was ſo late when he
arrived there, and the Perſon who opened the Gate, was ſo ſleepy, that he could
ſcarce prevail with him to furniſh him
with a Light. He went up directly to
his Apartment, to which he always had
a Key; juſt as he open'd the Door, the
Light went out: However, pulling off
his Cloaths, he got into Bed as faſt as he
could.

BUT what was his ſurpriſe when he
perceiv'd he was not alone, and found,
by the Delicateneſs of a Foot which
reſted itſelf upon him, that he was in
Bed with a Woman! He was young,
and not inſenſible. This Adventure,
which

which paſt his Underſtanding, had already given him not a little Emotion, when this Woman, who was ſtill aſleep, drew near to him in ſuch Sort, that he was enabled to judge very advantageouſly of the Beauty of her Perſon.

SUCH Moments are no Moments of Reflection; accordingly the Count *de Canaple* made none, but ſeiz'd the good Fortune which offer'd itſelf to him. This Perſon, who was all the while between ſleeping and waking, fell again immediately into a profound Sleep; but no Reſpect was paid to her Repoſe. O my GOD! ſaid ſhe, with a Voice full of Charms, why won't you let me ſleep! The Voice of Madam *de Granſon*, which the Count *de Canaple* knew perfectly well, threw him into ſuch Trouble, Diſorder and Perturbation of Mind as he had never experienced before. He crept back again to his former Place, and, with a Fear which almoſt depriv'd him of Breath, waited for the Moment when
he

he could get away. At laſt he got a-
way, and ſo happily as not to be ſeen
by any Body, and quickly reacht Mr. *de
Chalon*'s Houſe.

EXTASY and Rapture immediately
took entire Poſſeſſion of him. Madam
de Granſon preſented herſelf to his imagination, with all her Charms; he reproach'd himſelf for not having had a
Senſe of them: He beg'd her Pardon for
it (to himſelf.) What have I been doing
all this while? ſaid he. Ah! how well
would I compenſate for the Time I have
loſt, by the Ardency of my future Behaviour! But, added he, will you forgive my Indifference; will you forget
that I could ſee you without adoring
you?

REASON at laſt reſum'd her Place,
and made him ſenſible of his Misfortune.
He ſaw, with Aſtoniſhment and Terror,
that he had betray'd his Friend, and done
the greateſt Injury to a Woman, whom

he

he now refpected far above what he had ever done. His very Soul was wounded; he was torn to Pieces with a Shame and Remorfe, which he had never felt before. He could not endure the Light, he could not tell what to do with himfelf; that Honour, of which he had made fuch nice Profeffion, rofe up againft him, exaggerated to him his Crime, and allow'd him no Excufe.

I HAVE, faid he, deferv'd the Hatred of the Only Woman I could love. How can I prefume to appear before her? Shall I go and make her blufh for *my* Guilt? No; I muft go far away for ever, and give her, by condemning myfelf to an eternal Abfence, the only Satisfaction I can give her.

THIS Refolution held not long. Love recover'd its Empire, and the very Reflecting on the Crime, which he detefted, did, in fpite of himfelf, adminifter fome Degree of Eafe to his Soul, by bringing certain

certain pleasing Ideas along with it; he entertain'd some Hopes that he should never be known. But if this Thought comforted him, it made him not the bolder. How shall he dare to look her in the Face with such a Load of conscious Guilt upon him?

MADAM *de Granson* did not wake till a long While after the Count *de Canaple* was gone. She had been obliged to relinquish her Apartment to the Countess *d'Artois*, who had stopt there in her Way to an Estate she had in that Neighbourhood. Mr. *de Granson*, before the Arrival of the Countess *d'Artois*, was call'd abroad by a very urgent Affair; but he had assur'd his Wife he would be back again the same Night: She thought her Servants had told their Master where she lay, and that this had made him come to her in Mr. *de Canaple*'s Apartment. As she was going to rise, she perceiv'd something in her Bed, which sparkled; and saw, with Surprise, that it

was

was the Stone of a Ring, which had been given by his Majesty (*Philip de Valois*) to Mr. *de Canaple*, in Reward of his Valor; and which he never omitted to wear. Quite stunn'd, as it were, struck thro' with surprise, and fixt in Amazement at this Sight, she knew not what to think. The Suspicions which crowded into her Mind, sunk her down with Grief. However, there still remain'd to her some Uncertainty; but Mr. *de Granson*'s Arrival left her not that, very long.

HE came in the Morning; and came in the most indearing Manner, begging a thousand Pardons for not keeping his Promise to her. What a Thunder-stroke was here! her Misfortune, now no longer doubtful, appear'd to her such as it really was; the Paleness of her Face, and an universal Trembling which seiz'd her, made Mr. *de Granson* apprehensive she was sick; he askt her, with Inquietude, how it far'd with her, and prest

her

her to go to bed again. Inftead of giving ear to him, fhe hurry'd out from a Place, which, in fo forcible, fo flagrant a Manner, recall'd her Shame to mind.

THE Countefs *d'Artois* refolv'd upon going away that fame Morning, and Madam *de Granfon* us'd no endeavours to hinder her. Mr. *de Granfon* thinking it became him to wait on the Countefs home, his Abfence gave Madam *de Granfon* the fad, the melancholy Liberty of giving herfelf up to her Sorrow; and indeed there never was a greater: She faw herfelf injur'd in the moft cruel Manner, by a Man whom fhe had the Weaknefs to love. She fancy'd herfelf defpis'd by him, and this Thought created in her fo much Refentment againft him, that fhe now hated him as much as fhe had lov'd him before.

How! faid fhe, the Man that was afraid he fhould forfeit his Honour, if

he

he let a Woman believe he lov'd her;
does this Man cease to be virtuous towards Me alone! Could I, amidst my
Misfortunes, but have the Hope of a-
venging myself! — But I must stifle my
Resentment, to conceal the shameful
Cause of it. What would become of
me, great GOD! should this fatal Secret
be seen into!

SHE spent the Day and Night, buried
in an Abyss of Grief. Her Husband return'd the next Morning, and with him
several Persons of Quality, whose Promises he had got to come and see him.
Madam *de Beaumont* was of the Number.
In any other Circumstance, Madam *de
Granson* would have seen her with Pleasure; but Madam *de Beaumont* was Sister
to Mr. *de Canaple*; her Presence redoubled the Confusion of Madam *de
Granson*. For a Completion of it, she
askt her Friend News of her Brother;
Madam *de Granson* answered, blushing
and with a faltring Accent, that he was

not

not at her Houfe ; and haften'd to other
Difcourfe.

IT was not a long While before Madam *de Beaumont* took Notice of the
deep Melancholy wherein her Friend
was plung'd. Why will you not tell
me what it is that afflicts you fo much ?
faid fhe to her, one Day when fhe found
her bath'd in Tears. I don't know,
myfelf, anfwer'd Madam *de Granfon* ;
Madam *de Beaumont* again repeated her
Requeft, but finding it only increaft her
Friend's Uneafinefs, fhe forbore preffing her any further.

MR. *de Canaple* having now been abfent fome Time, Mr. *de Granfon* writ to
him to haften his Return. The former
concluded from thence, that Madam *de
Granfon* ftill remain'd in Ignorance ; and
being fpurr'd up with a Defire to fee her
again, he fet immediately out ; but the
nearer he drew, the more his Hopes va-
nifh'd, and his Fears increaft ; and had

he

he not been met by one of the Domeſtics, he had, perhaps, return'd to the
Place from whence he came.

HE arrived, ſo diſmay'd, ſo very
much out of Order, that he could hardly
ſupport himſelf. Every one was engaged at Play; only Madam *de Granſon*
ſat by herſelf in a Corner of the Room
in a very melancholy Manner, and with
a clouded Brow: He went to her with a
tottering Step, and without daring to
look her in the Face, pronounced ſome
broken, indiſtinct Words with a diſorder'd and timorous Voice. The Trouble
ſhe herſelf was in, did not ſuffer her to
give Attention to that of the Count *de
Canaple.*

THEY both kept Silence, when ſhe
let fall a Piece of Work ſhe was upon;
He immediately took it up, and as he
was preſenting it to her, his Hand happen'd to touch Madam *de Granſon*'s; ſhe
haſtily drew it back, and caſt a look at him
full

full of Indignation. Fell'd to the
Ground with this Blow, no Thunder-
bolt could have ftruck him more forely.
Sunk into moft deep Defpair, and being
no longer Mafter of his Mind ; he went
and fhut himfelf up in his Chamber.
This Place, where he had been fo happy, did, in vain, recall agreeable Images,
he felt nothing but the Misfortune of
being hated.

THE Manner in which Madam *de
Granfon* look'd at him, her confus'd Behaviour, her Silence, every Thing fhew'd
that fhe knew the Crime he had committed. Alas! faid he, did fhe but likewife
know my Repentance! — But I am not
fo much as permitted to fhew it her; I
am not permitted to die at her Feet.
How little did I know the Nature of
Love, when I thought it only fubfifted
by the Help of Defire! It is not the
Felicity I have enjoy'd which I lament ;
that, to me, is nothing, unlefs the
Heart had accompanied it and given a

C　　　　　Relifh

Relish to the Gift: One Look would make me happy. He then resolv'd, by his Respect and Submission, to make Madam *de Granson* forget what was past, and to behave himself so as she might flatter herself with Hopes that *He* had forgot it too. The Friendship which was between him and Mr. *de Granson*, threw no Obstacle in the Way of this Design. The Point he aim'd at was not To be Belov'd, he only aim'd at Not being Hated.

MADAM *de Beaumont*, who was gone abroad to take the Air, at her Return being told her Brother was come, she flew to find him out. They ask'd each other what had happen'd since they parted: And this was the first Time that ever the Count *de Canaple* dissembled with a Sister whom he fondly lov'd.

HE would have given way to a Desire of speaking concerning Madam *de Granson*, had he not felt that it was impossible

poffible for him to pronounce that Name
in the Manner he was wont to do.
Madam *de Beaumont* prevented the Queftion which he was afraid to put to her.
You have been fuccefsful in your Endea-
deavours, faid fhe to him; *Granfon* is
more in love with his Wife than ever he
was. She is then well pleas'd, faid Mr.
de Canaple with a Diforder he had much
ado to conceal. I don't know what is
the Matter, reply'd Madam *de Beaumont*,
fhe loves her Hufband, fhe is beloved
by him; and yet fhe has a fecret Sadnefs which preys upon her, and even
extorts Tears from her.

THESE Words pierced Mr. *de Canaple*
to the Heart. He but too plainly faw he
was the Author of thofe Tears; and the
Jealoufy which began to arife in his
Heart againft a Hufband that was lov'd,
fill'd the Meafure of his Defperation.
He would gladly have continu'd alone,
but he was obliged to go to the Company again. In fpite of all he could do,

C 2 there

there fat fuch a Sorrow and Dejection on his Countenance, that Madam *de Granfon* could not but obferve it, and her own Affliction was thereby in fome Degree diminifh'd.

SUPPER was ferv'd; after which the Night was fpent in different Diverfions; and, as Fortune would have it, Mr. *de Canaple* always happen'd to be placed near Madam *de Granfon.* He could not hinder his Eyes from rivetting themfelves on her; but he caft them down with a timorous Air whenever fhe perceived it, and he feem'd to afk her Pardon for his Audacioufnefs.

HE call'd to Mind that fhe had formerly writ him fome Letters, which he had kept. The Impatience he was in to read them over again, did not permit him to ftay 'till he return'd to *Dijon.* He fent a Valet de Chambre to fetch the Cafket in which he had put them. The Letters appear'd to him far different

ferent

ferent from what they seem'd to him before: Although they contain'd nothing
but Trifles, he could not read them o-
ver often enough; the Teſtimonies of
Friendſhip which occur'd therein, gave
him at firſt a ſenſible Pleaſure, but this
Pleaſure was of no long Duration; it
only ſerv'd to make him feel, with more
Severity, the different Treatment he
now met with.

Madam *de Granſon* was, however,
not quite ſo much incens'd againſt him;
his reſpectful Behaviour to her wrought
its Effect by little and little; but it did
not leſſen either her Shame or Perplexity
of Mind; it might poſſibly add even
ſomewhat to them; but what increas'd
them to the Height was the over ardent
Officiouſneſs of Mr. *de Granſon*, and his
vehement Uxoriouſneſs before Company.
It put her Modeſty to no ſmall Difficulties to anſwer his Fondneſs; and not
to anſwer it, had been a Kind of Fa-
vor to the Count *de Canaple*, who was

C 3   oftentimes

oftentimes an Eye-witness of thofe En-
dearments.

How great were his Sufferings on
fuch Occafions! He fometimes went out
of Madam *de Granfon*'s Chamber, fo o-
vercome with Defpair that he fully refolv'd never to enter it any more. I
have thrown myfelf into this Abyfs,
would he fay, had it not been for me,
had it not been for my medling, *Granfon*, a Slave to his Inconftancy, would
have given fuch Difguft to his Wife,
that fhe would have ceas'd to love him,
and I had been, at leaft, deliver'd from
the Torment of feeing her kind to another Man. But (taking himfelf up)
would he fay again; have I forgot that
this Man, who excites my Jealoufy, is
my Friend? Would I rob him of the
Sweets of his marriage? Is it poffible
my Paffion fhould bewilder me to that
Pitch? I no longer know any other
Sentiments, any other Refpects but thefe
of Love. My little Share of Virtue,
whatever

whatever it was, which I had, is now ravish'd from me by this fatal Passion; and instead of opposing it, I study how to cherish it; I frame to myself vain pretences to see Madam *de Granson*, whom I ought of all Things to avoid seeing. I must remove far from her, and regain, if I can, that happy Situation wherein I may be alone, wherein I may, with Satisfaction, get acquainted with the Depths of my own Soul.

MR. *de Canaple* was not the only Person who took the like Resolution; it was to avoid him that Madam *de Granson* was come into the Country, and the same Motive urg'd her to return again to *Dijon*.

MADAM *de Beaumont* and the rest of the Company went away some Days before that which Madam *de Granson* had fix'd for her Departure. None but the Count *de Canaple* was left. He thought that as he design'd to shun the Sight of Madam *de*

Granson

Granfon for ever, he might allow himfelf the Satisfaction of feeing her two
Days more. She took the utmoft Care
to decline being prefent where he was.
And though he long'd to be in her company, he was too fearful of himfelf to
feek an Opportunity of being in it.

CHANCE brought about that which
he did not dare to do. The Day before
that which was fet for their Departure,
he went and took a Walk in a Grove
near the Houfe; and after he had been
there a confiderable Time, he difcover'd
Madam *de Granfon* fitting on a green
Bank fome Paces from him. Without
fo much as knowing what he did, he ad-
vanc'd towards her: The Sight of Mr.
de Canaple fo near her, made her ftart;
and rifing up with an affrighted Air,
fhe convey'd herfelf away with all Speed.
Inftead of endeavouring to ftop her
Flight, Amazement and Confufion had
render'd him motionlefs; and Mr. *de
Granfon,* who was in queft of him in order

der to impart to him some Letters he had just receiv'd, found him still in the same Place, so wrapt in Thougnt, that he ask'd him more than once, in vain, what he did there.

AT last he answer'd, as well as he was able; but Mr. *de Granson*, intent upon his Letters, gave no Heed to his Answer. The Truce, said he to him, is newly broke between *France* and *England*. Mr. *de Vienne*, my Father-in-law, is appointed Governor of *Calais*; *Edward* is thought to have a Design on *Picardy*, and the whole Stress of the War will be on that Side. It would ill become me to stay at home, whilst all *France* shall be in Arms; I have a Desire to offer my Service to the King; but as my Father-in-law, who has Orders to set out for his Government, cannot present me to his Majesty, I promise myself that Piece of Service from your Friendship.

SUCH

SUCH a Man as you, reply'd the Count *de Canaple,* carries his own Recommendation along with him; however I will do whatever fhall fuit you; but if you are minded we fhould go to Court together, we have not a Moment to lofe. The Company of *Gens d'Armes,* which I have the Honour to command, is actually in *Picardy.* I will leave you to judge of the Concern it would give me if, during my Abfence, any Action fhould happen. I afk but two Days of you, faid Mr. *de Granfon.* I will go, reply'd the Count *de Canaple,* and wait for you at *Dijon,* where I have fome Bufinefs to fettle.

THE Count *de Canaple* who, after what had juft fallen out, dreaded to fee Madam *de Granfon,* found a Sort of Confolation in his being neceffitated to depart. But he had quite other Thoughts when at his Arrival at her Houfe, he was inform'd that, under the Pretext

of

of an Indifpofition, fhe was gone to
Bed, and had order'd nobody fhould enter her Chamber. This Order, which
he was but too fenfible was level'd at
him, wounded his very Soul. Could I
but have feen her, faid he, my Sorrow would have told her what my
Tongue is not able to tell her. Peradventure fhe accufes me of Boldnefs; fhe
might at leaft have read in my Eyes,
and in my whole Deportment, how far
I am from it. Abfence feem'd to me
fupportable, no farther than as it was a
Mark of my Refpect; it is only at that
Price that I can refolve upon it. It
is at leaft neceffary that Madam *de Granfon* fhould know I fly from her, in order to impofe on myfelf the Laws which
She would impofe on me, did fhe vouchfafe to give me any.

HE could not refolve with himfelf to
get away; he was in Hopes Mr. *de
Granfon* would go into his Wife's A-
partment, and that he might follow
C 6   him;

him; but Madam *de Granfon*, who fear'd the very Thing which Mr. *de Canaple* hop'd, fent to defire her Hufband to leave her to her Repofe.

AT laft, after he had done all he could, he was forc'd to depart without feeing her. The Company of *Gens d'Armes*, commanded by Mr. *de Chalons*, was likewife in *Picardy*. The Count *de Canaple* refolv'd to go to his Friend to inform him what he had juft learn'd; Mr. *de Chalons* was not at home, he came in late and detain'd the Count *de Canaple* fo long, that he could not fet out before the next Morning.

He had travel'd Part of the Day, when going up a Hill, one of his Servants made him take Notice of a Chariot in Mr. *de Granfon*'s Livery, which the Horfes were dragging, with great Violence, down the Defcent of a fteep Hill. He foon knew the Voice of her whofe Shriekings he heard: It was that

of

of Madam *de Granſon*. He flew to the
Head of the Horſes; and after he had
ſtopped them, he went to the Chariot,
where he ſaw Madam *de Granſon*: She
was fallen into a Swoon. He took her
in his Arms, and laid her on a little
Hillock of green Turf. All her Attendants, being buſied in putting the
Chariot to Rights, or in going to fetch
Relief at a neighbouring Houſe, left
Mr. *de Canaple* with their Lady. He
was there alone. She was between his
Arms. What a Moment was here,
could he but have reliſhed the Sweets
of it! But it was taſteleſs and inſipid to
him, becauſe he owed to Fortune alone
the Happineſs which he poſſeſſed. Madam *de Granſon*'s Conſent was wanting.

SHE came to herſelf again, juſt as
thoſe who went for Relief were come
back; and, without turning her Eyes
on the Count *de Canaple*, ſhe aſked for
ſome Water. He haſtened to preſent
her ſome. She then knew him; and at
firſt

first she resolved to refuse it: But the Sadness and deep Concern which she saw in his Eyes did not leave her the Power to do it. She took what he presented to her. This Favour, which was only so on account of the first Refusal, infused such a Joy into the Soul of the Count *de Canaple* as he never experienced before. Madam *de Granson* reproached herself for what she had done. Being utterly at a loss what she should say, she kept Silence; when Mr. *de Granson* coming up, still heightened the Hurry of her Spirits. She left it to him to thank Mr. *de Canaple* for the Assistance she had received from him; and, without lifting up her Eyes, without uttering a Word, she got into her Chariot again.

Mr. *de Canaple*, who was no longer supported by the Pleasure of seeing Madam *de Granson*, now found he had been hurt in stopping the Horses. Mr. *de Granson* perceiving it to be a great Pain

Pain to Mr. *de Canaple* to ride on Horfeback, propofed to him to go into the Chariot with his Wife. But, whatever Pleafure he might have found in being many Hours with Madam *de Granfon*, the Fear he had of difpleafing her, and putting her into Perplexities, created in him Refolution enough to refufe a Thing which he would have accepted of at the Expence of his Life.

MADAM *de Granfon* was, all the whole Journey, in a Chaos of Thoughts and Sentiments, which fhe did not dare to examine. She would have been glad, had it been poffible for her, to have forgot both the Offences and the Services of the Count *de Canaple*. The Accident which had befallen her, by furnifhing her with a Pretence for keeping her Bed, excufed her from feeing him.

THE

THE Character which Mr. *de Canaple* gave of Mr. *de Granson*, when he presented him to the King, occasioned that Prince to bestow on him some pleasing Distinctions. As soon as Mr. *de Canaple* conceived himself to be no longer necessary to the Service of his Friend, he went into *Picardy* to rejoin his Troop. Mr. *de Chalons*, spurred up with a Desire which was no less powerful than that of Glory, had got thither before him. They had appointed to meet at *Boulogne*. Mr. *de Canaple* was surprized at his not finding him there, and to hear he had stopt there but a Moment, and nobody knew where he was. Uneasy for his Friend, whose Absence in the present Juncture might prejudice his Fortune, he was going to send to *Calais*, where he was told he might hear of him; when a Man belonging to Mr. *de Chalons* came and desired he would go to him to a Place which he shewed him.

MR.

MR. *de Canaple* was furprized to find Mr. *de Chalons* in his Bed, and to hear he was wounded. He was going to aſk him how it happened; but Mr. *de Chalons* prevented his Queſtions. I am under a Neceſſity of having your Aſſiſtance, ſaid he to him, in the moſt preſſing Occaſion of my Life. Do not, however, think, my dear *Canaple*, that it is to this Neceſſity you owe my making you my Confident. I would have told you in *Burgundy*, what I am now going to tell you, had not your Severity in Matters of Gallantry and Love reſtrained me. You are to be blamed, ſaid Mr. *de Canaple*, for fearing what you call my Severity: I condemn Love, only becauſe Men make ſo ſlight a Matter of it, that it always ends in a bad Uſage of the Women. You ſhall judge, replied Mr. *de Chalons*, whether I deſerve any Reproaches of that kind.

MY

MY Father, about two Years. ago, sent me into *Picardy*, to take Possession of an Estate of my Mother's. I was at a Seat, which belonged to her, situated at some Distance from *Calais*. Business did not fill up all my Time : I sought out Amusements suitable to my Age and Humour. A Gentleman, one of my Neighbours, carried me to the Count *de Mailly*, who was spending the Autumn at an Estate not far from mine. He did his utmost to make me welcome; but the Beauty of Mademoiselle *de Mailly*, his Daughter, who was with him, might have spared him the Trouble. I never beheld Features more regular, and, what rarely meets in the same Person, a more agreeable Behaviour. Her Wit was answerable to her external Figure; and I thought the Beauty of her Soul superior to both. I loved her as soon as I saw her; nor was it long before I told her so. But, though she has since often flattered me, that

that her Heart did at the very firſt declare itſelf for me, I had not the Pleaſure of hearing her tell me ſo, till after
my Paſſion was approved of by Mr. *de
Mailly.*

NOTHING but my Father's Conſent
was wanting to my Happineſs. I prepared to go and aſk it of him ; and
being ſure of obtaining it, I departed
without affecting a Sadneſs which I did
not feel. It was almoſt not leaving
Mademoiſelle *de Mailly* at all, the going to take Order never to leave her. I
told her ingenuouſly my Thoughts. I
am not at all ſurprized at them, ſaid
ſhe ; the Buſineſs you are going about,
and of which I am the Object, will be
the ſame thing to you as if I was with
you : But my Situation is very different ; I am going to be without you,
and ſhall be doing nothing for you.

MY Father received my Propoſal of
Marriage as I hoped and expected he
would,

would, and even prepared to set out with me. But all our Schemes were overturned by a Letter he received from the King. This Prince notified to him, that he was going to reduce the *Flemings* to their Duty ; that he had Occasion for the Assistance of his good Servants : He ordered him to repair to him, and bring me along with him ; that, designing him for more important Employments, he would bestow on me the Company of *Gens d'Arms*, which my Father then commanded.

THE Movements of the Army, which was getting together from all Parts, allowed us not to make any Delay in our Departure ; and, notwithstanding the Grief it gave me, I could not but give the Preference to the Calls of Honour and Duty. I wrote to the Count *de Mailly* the Necessity I was under of deferring my Marriage till my Return from *Flanders*, and the Pain which that Delay gave me. What did I not say

to

to his Daughter! This Abſence, very different from the former, offered me no Compenſation, but left me a Prey to my whole Grief; and there never was a more piercing one; and if the Fear of making myſelf unworthy of her I loved, had not ſupported me, I ſhould never have had Strength enough to ſepa-rate myſelf from her. The Anſwers which I received from *Calais* gave new Additions to my Love.

THE Battle of *Caſſel*, wherein you acquired ſo much Glory, coſt me my Father. I was greatly afflicted at this Loſs, and went and ſought, at Made-moiſelle *de Mailly's*, the only Conſola-tion I could have. I had not heard from her a conſiderable Time; which I imputed to the Difficulty of getting her Letters conveyed to me; and there-fore felt on that Account no other ſort of Uneaſineſs but what is natural to thoſe who are in Love. I flew to *Calais*, where I had been informed ſhe was
with

with Mr. *de Mailly*. I found her at home all alone; but, instead of the Joy which I expected, she received me with Tears.

I CANNOT express to you how much I was troubled at it. You weep! said I exclaiming. Great God! what am I to learn from these Tears? You are to learn from them, answered she, still weeping, That our Fortune is changed, and that my Heart is not. Ah! replied I, with Emotion, Mr. *de Mailly* has then altered his Mind, and is for breaking his Engagements to me. My Father, replied she, is more to be pitied than blamed: Attend, and promise you will not hate him.

SOME time after your Departure he fell into the Company of Madam *de Boulai*. Although she is not very young, she has still the Freshness and florid Agreeableness of Youth. The artful Manner in which she had lived with a

Husband

Hufband of an Age very different from hers, and of a Temper difficult enough to deal with, procured her the Efteem of all fuch as judge only by Appearances. Together with thefe Advantages, fhe has a moft infinuating and deluding Wit. Abfolute Miftrefs of her Inclinations and Sentiments, fhe has only fuch as are of Ufe to her.

My Father, whofe Soul is apt to take an Impreffion, efpecially of Love, conceived a Paffion for her, and made a Propofal of Marriage to her. I have a Son whom I love, anfwered fhe, and who, by his Birth and perfonal Qualities, is worthy of Mademoifelle *de Mailly:* If you love me as much as you fay you do, you muft, in order to countenance my beftowing myfelf on you, refolve that we make but one and the fame Family.

My Father, who was deeply fmitten with her, continued Mademoifelle *de Mailly,* without remembering his En-

gagements

gagements to you, came and propoſed to me to marry Mr. *de Boulai.* The Grief which this Propoſal gave me, revived all his Tenderneſs for me: He did not diſguiſe to me the Violence of his Paſſion; he concluded with telling me, he would never conſtrain me; and that, if I conſented to his Happineſs, he would wholly owe that Sacrifice to my Friendſhip, and not to my Obedience. This is the Circumſtance I am in. He ſays nothing to me; but his Sorrow, which I but too plainly ſee, ſays more to me than he could ſay himſelf. One of us two muſt ſacrifice their Happineſs to the Happineſs of the other. Is it my Father that ought to make this Sacrifice? and ought I to exact it?

I ANSWERED Mademoiſelle *de Mailly* no otherwiſe than by the Tokens of my Deſpair. I judged myſelf to be no longer loved by her. I will now, ſaid ſhe, make you fully ſenſible how unjuſt

you

you are, and give you a fresh Proof of
the Esteem I have for you. You see
my Situation; you love me; you know
I love you; decide your own Lot and
mine: but take four and twenty Hours
to resolve yourself.

SHE quitted me at these Words, and
left me in a Condition which you may
easily judge. The more I loved her,
the more I feared to engage her in Measures which might hazard her Reputation and Repose. I knew how dear her
Father was to her; I knew that her
Father's Unhappiness would become hers.
After the four and twenty Hours she
had given me were past, I re-visited her,
without having the Resolution to make
myself either happy or miserable. And
so we parted, without coming to any
Determination.

A FEW Days after this, she gave me
an Account of a Conversation she had
had with her Father. He renounced the

D   Authority

Authority Nature had given him ; and
made it thereby the stronger : He employed only Entreaties to his Daughter.
You are more prudent than I, said he to
her ; endeavour to triumph over your
Inclinations ; prevail on yourself to be,
for a Time, without seeing Mr. *de Chalons :* If after that you continue in the
same Mind, I promise you, and I promise myself, I will leave you to your
Liberty.   I cannot, said Mademoiselle
de Mailly to me, refuse my Father what
he is pleased to ask of me, and what he
might command of me.   As I am no
Hypocrite, I will farther own to you,
that I will do my Endeavours to obey
him.   I am sensible they will be in
vain : You are very powerful in my
Heart, since you prevail above my Father.   Ah ! cried I, you no longer love
me ; seeing you form a Design of no
longer loving me.   Mademoiselle *de
Mailly* made no other Answer to my
Chidings, than by the Grief with which
I plainly saw she was pierced.   We continued

tinued thus a confiderable time together;
we were not able to part. She at laft
ordered me to be gone, and to leave the
Care of our Fortune to her. I hope,
faid fhe to me, I fhall find a Way
to fatisfy all the Sentiments of my
Heart.

I WAS forced to obey. I went into
Burgundy; where I heard, fome Months
after, that Madam *de Boulai* was married
to Mr. *de Mailly.* I was to the laft degree furprifed, that Mademoifelle *de
Mailly* had given me no Intimation of
fuch Marriage. This Way of Proceeding, which was paft my Comprehenfion,
gave me fome Inquietude and Pain, but
no Sufpicion.

I HAD promifed her, to take no Step
but in Concert with her: But, as I had
received no News, I determined to go
to *Calais incognito.* As eager as I was
to put this Defign in Execution, I was
forced to obey an Order which the King

gave

gave me to go to *Gant*, and confer with the Earl of *Flanders*. As soon as the Bufinefs I went about was finifhed, I took the Road to *Calais*. I fixed my Lodging in a By-place, and fent out, for Intelligence, one whofe Fidelity I had experienced, a Man of Senfe and Dexterity.

In a few Days he brought me Intelligence, that Mr. *de Boulai* was deeply in love with Mademoifelle *de Mailly* ; that he was jealous of her ; that the affiduous Services of my Lord *Arundel*, who had appeared very fond of Mademoifelle *de Mailly* during the Stay he had made at *Calais*, had given him much Uneafinefs, and no lefs Jealoufy ; that Mr. *de Mailly* was gone out of Town with his whole Family.

I knew my Lord *Arundel* to be one of the moft amiable Men in the World ; he was in love with my Miftrefs, and this Miftrefs feemed to have neglected

me

me for a long time paſt.   Needed there
any thing more to create a Jealouſy in
me? Notwithſtanding their telling me,
that Mademoiſelle *de Mailly* was not at
Calais, my Reſtleſsneſs carried me into
the Street where ſhe lived. It was
Night; and a profound Silence reigned
in the Houſe. I perceived, however,
a Light in Mademoiſelle *de Mailly's*
Apartment: I concluded, ſhe was not
gone away; that perhaps ſhe was alone;
and that, by the means of ſome Dome-
ſtick, it was not impoſſible but I might
be introduced to her. The Pleaſure
which I ſhould have in ſeeing her again,
after ſo long an Abſence, employed my
Thoughts ſo entirely, that it took place
of the Jealouſy I had lately conceived:
And now that Door, on which I had
ſteadily fixed my Eyes, was opened;
and out of it I ſaw a Woman come;
who, notwithſtanding the Darkneſs of
the Night, I knew to be a Domeſtic of
Mademoiſelle *de Mailly*.

I AD-

I ADVANCED towards her: it seemed to me as if she knew me; but, instead of staying for me, she hastened away with all Speed. The Desire I had to get an Insight into a Procedure which astonished me, and to know what obliged her to go out at so unseasonable an an Hour, engaged me to follow her. After crossing some Streets, she went into a House; out of which she came again a Moment after with another Woman, and returned to Mr. *de Mailly's* House. I still followed her; and withal kept so close to them, that he who opened the Door to them, certainly thought that I belonged to them; and so let me go in.

THEY went directly to Mademoiselle *de Mailly's* Apartment: They were in such a Hurry, they took no Notice of me; I could even have gone into the Chamber: But, though it was now shut, it was easy for me to perceive there was

something

something extraordinary in Agitation. I was racking my Thoughts what it could be; when the Cries which I heard from time to time, which were followed a Moment after by those of a young Child, cleared up to me this strange Mystery. I cannot describe to you what passed within my own Breast at that Time; so violent a State of Mind admits of nothing but confused Ideas. The Beating of my Heart, the Excess of my Trouble and of my Dismay, were what I was most sensible of.

THE Woman whom I had seen go in with Mademoiselle *de Mailly*'s Servant, went out. I followed her, without having any settled Purpose, or determined Design : She carried with her the Child which was newly born. Those who go the Rounds in fortified Places, were then passing by. I knew not whether it was that she was afraid of being known by them, or whether it was in Execution of her Orders; but she no sooner

D 4   perceived

perceived them coming, but she laid down the Child at a Door, and got away into a By-street.

IT was not of me that this little Creature was to expect Relief; however it did not go without it, through a Sentiment of Pity, mixed with a kind of relenting Softness for the Mother. Besides, I thought it a sort of avenging myself on her, to have her Child in my Power. I put it into the Hands of the Woman where I lodged, and went and shut myself up in my Chamber, quite swallowed up in Thought. The more I revolved this Adventure in my Mind, the less I comprehended it. My Heart was so accustomed to love and esteem Mademoiselle *de Mailly*, it was so difficult for me to think her guilty, that I gave no Credit to my Ears and Eyes. She could not possibly betray me : she could not possibly be wanting to herself. I concluded there

was

was something in all this which I did not understand.

I WAS forming a Resolution of getting Light into this Secret, when the Woman to whom I had just committed this little Creature, through a Persuasion that I was its Father, brought it to me, to let me see, she said, what a wonderful pretty Child it was. Although I turned away my Face with Horror, I know not how I perceived it was covered with a Mantle, made of a foreign Stuff which I had given Mademoiselle *de Mailly.* What a Sight was this, my dear *Canaple !* and what did it not produce in me ! I seemed not to know I was betrayed till after that Moment : Every thing I had before been thinking of, vanished away. I rejected, with Indignation, Doubts which had in some degree suspended my Grief. Then it became extreme, and my Resentment was proportioned to it ; perhaps I had given a Loose to it, if a

D 5   singular

fingular Event, which obliged me to leave *Calais* the very next Day, had not given my Reafon Time to refume its Empire.

IT is impoffible for me to paint out to you the Condition I was in; I brooded over my Sorrow; my Heart found it was neceffitated to love. I found myfelf more unhappy in renouncing a State fo fevere, than I was in having been betrayed. In fhort, being far lefs incenfed than afflicted, all my Thoughts tended to juftify Mademoifelle *de Mailly.* I could have no Peace with myfelf, but when I was arrived fo far as to form Doubts. I wrote to her, and reproached her: My Reproaches were accompanied with a Refpect which I ftill felt for her, and from which a Man of Honour can never difpenfe with himfelf to a Woman he has once loved. My Letter was faithfully delivered; but, inftead of the Anfwer which I expected,

it

it was fent me back again, without fo much as being opened.

THE Indignation with which this Mark of Contempt infpired my Breaft, made me enter upon a Refolution to triumph over my Love; a Refolution which I had not taken till then, or which at leaft I had taken but feebly. In order to fucceed the better therein, I threw myfelf again into the World, which I had almoft quitted. I vifited Women; I was defirous to think them beautiful; I hunted for Charms in them: But, in fpite of all I could do, my Mind and my Heart ftill made Comparifons which threw me back into my former Chains.

WE repaired, You and I, to our Troop. As foon as I was within Reach of Mademoifelle *de Mailly*, the Defire of feeing her, and of clearing up my Doubts, awaked in my Heart. It runs in my Mind, fhe's married; and that,

D 6   for

for some Reason which I am a Stranger to, she is obliged to conceal it. The Child, which I have in my Power, and which I saw exposed, does not over-well agree with this Notion; but my Heart stands in need of Esteeming that which it cannot forbear Loving.

I HAVE been three whole Nights at *Calais:* The two first I spent in walking round Mr. *de Mailly's* House; I was set upon the third Night by three Men, who attacked me Sword in Hand. I presently drew mine; and, to prevent their taking me behind, I clapped my Back against a Wall. One of my three Adversaries was soon disabled. I had till then only stood upon the defensive; but now I resolved to attack; and was so fortunate, that my last Enemy, after receiving several Wounds, fell bathed in his Blood: I lost a good deal myself; and finding my Strength fail, I hastened to the Place where a Man whom I had with me waited for me.

He

He ftanched the Blood as well as he could. My Wounds are not thought dangerous; and if my Mind would allow me to reft a little, I fhould foon be well : But, inftead of that, a Letter which I received yefterday, here it is, throws me into a new Trouble, and a new Affliction.

This Letter, which Mr. *de Canaple* took out of his Friend's Hands, was conceived in the following Terms.

L E T T E R.

LOSE not a Moment's Time, but get away from a Place where there is a Conspiracy to destroy you. I should, perhaps, have sided with your Enemies; but, in spite of your Treachery, I still remember I have loved you ; and I feel that my Indifference towards you will be more assured, when I shall have nothing to fear for your Life.

I TREA-

I TREACHEROUS! cried Mr. *de Chalons*, when Mr. *de Canaple* had done
reading the Letter; and is it Mademoifelle *de Mailly* that accufes me of it!
She will have me be guilty! She will
have it, that I never truly loved her!
Do you comprehend, added he, the
Species of Pain which I feel? No; you
do not comprehend it: One muft love,
before he can know, that the greateft
Pain of Love is that of not being able to
perfuade that one does love. Alas! perhaps I am only played falfe with by way
of Revenge! Great God! how happy
fhould I be! Every thing would be par-
donable, every thing would be forgot,
could I but think I have always been
beloved! I cannot live in the Situation I
am in. You muft, my dear *Canaple*, go
to *Calais*; you muft fpeak with Máde-
moifelle *de Mailly*; your Name will eafily gain you Admittance into her Father's Houfe; but fay nothing to her
that may offend her: I fhould die with
Grief,

Grief, if I expofed her to blufh before you: I would only have it be made known to her, to what a Degiee I ftill love her.

THE Count *de Canaple*, who, from his own Experience, was become yet more fenfible of his Friend's Grief, fet out for *Calais*, after he had received fome more particular Inftructions.

End of the Firft Part.

THE

SIEGE of *CALAIS*,

BY

EDWARD of ENGLAND.

PART II.

MONSIEUR *de Canaple*, upon his Arrival at *Calais*, was inform'd that Mr. *du Boulai* was the Person with whom Mr. *de Chalons* had fought; that he was dead of his Wounds; that Madam *de Mailly* breath'd nothing but Revenge. This was no very proper Time to go to Mr. *de Mailly*'s; but a Man of such Merit and Rank as that of the Count *de Canaple*, was above the ordi-

nary

nary Rules. Madam *de Mailly*, taken wholly up with her Grief, left to Mademoiselle *de Mailly* the Care of performing the Honours of her House; in which, although she acquitted herself with much Politeness, yet she could not conceal her extreme Melancholly.

IF the Death of Mr. *de Boulai*, said the Count *de Canaple* to her after some Discourse, occasions the Sadness I see you in; I know an unhappy Man, a Thousand Times more unhappy, although he does not think he is. Pardon me, Madam, continued he (perceiving Mademoiselle *de Mailly*'s Surprise and Trouble) for being so well instructed; and pardon my Friend, for having confided his Sufferings to me, and charg'd me with an Eclaircissement, which, in the Condition he is in, he is not able to ask of you himself.

WHAT! answer'd she with a low and trembling Voice, is he then wounded?

ed? Yes, Madam, reply'd Mr. *de Canaple*; and, notwithstanding what he endures, he would be happy should he behold the Object I behold. Ah! said she with a Disquietness which she could not hide, he is wounded dangerously!

His Life, reply'd the Count *de Canaple*, depends on what you shall command me to say to him. Mademoiselle *de Mailly* was some Time in a deep Study, and without once lifting up her Eyes, which she still kept fix'd on the Ground; he has told you my Weaknesses, said she to him, but hath he acquainted you that at the very Time when I was resisting the Will of a Father, in order to preserve myself for him, he violated, in order to betray me, all the Laws both human and divine? Has he told you that he forc'd away Mademoiselle *de Liancourt*, that he fought with her Brother? What would he more? Why does he affect to spend whole Nights under my Windows? Why seek to trouble a Repose

pofe, which I have fo much trouble to regain? Why attack Mr. *de Boulai?* Why kill him? Why make his irreco-verable Enemies, all who ought to be moft dear to me? And laftly, why am I fo wretched as to fear, equal to Death itfelf, his being punifh'd for his Crimes? Yes, continu'd fhe, I dread, I tremble at the Meafures which Madam *de Mailly* is taking with Mr. *de Liancourt,* to de-ftroy this unhappy Man. Let him fly, let him fecure himfelf from the Hatred of his Enemies; let him live, and let me never fee him.

THIS laft Injunction, reply'd the Count *de Canaple,* puts him out of a Condition to obey you. Give me Time, Madam, to difcourfe him; I am fure he can't be guilty. Alas! what can he fay to you? reply'd fhe. No Matter, talk with him; I have already too much difcover'd my Weaknefs to you, to go about to hide from you the Uneafinefs and Dread which his Condition gives me.

MR.

MR. *de Chalons* waited for his Friend's Return, with an extreme Impatience. What are you going to tell me? said he to him, with a broken Speech, as soon as he saw him approaching to his Bed-side. That if the Suspicions which you entertain of Mademoiselle *de Mailly's* Constancy, reply'd Mr. *de Canaple*, have not been strong enough to quench your Love, she still loves you, although you are as guilty in her Eyes as she is in yours. What is that Battle you had with Mr. *de Liancourt*, and the Ravish-ment of his Sister, which you are accu-sed of; and to which I could say no-thing in your Justification? What I did for Mademoiselle *de Liancourt*, reply'd Mr. *de Chalons*, neither concerns my Love nor my Fidelity. I will let you into this Adventure in the fullest Manner; but prithee, dear *Canaple*, tell me more particularly all that was said to you; the most minute Circumstances, the Sound of her Voice, the Accent of

her

her Words, her Gestures, her Motions; every Thing is of Importance.

ALTHOUGH Mr. *de Canaple* made a most exact Recital of his late Conversation with Mademoiselle *de Mailly*, he still prest him for farther Particulars, he made no End of asking him Questions, he made him repeat the same Things a thousand Times over; and after all these Repetitions, he still fancy'd he had not distinctly heard them, or not rightly understood them. Shall I own my Pain to you? said he to him. I can't forgive myself the Suspicions which I have discovered to you; they may have made an Impression on you; you will have the less Esteem for Mademoiselle *de Mailly*; pray believe her not guilty, I beg it of you: As for myself, I have now almost no need of thinking so; nay, I do not know whether I should not feel a certain Pleasure in having her to pardon.

THIS

THIS Sentiment, which would have been so necessary to the Count *de Canaple* to find in Madam *de Granson*, made him sigh. You are in the right, said he to him; one pardons every Thing when one loves. Yes, reply'd Mr. *de Chalons*, but as I love sufficiently to pardon every Thing, so I have always too perfectly lov'd to stand in need of being pardon'd. You may remember that, as I was recounting to you the Adventures of that unhappy Night, I told you that a singular Event had oblig'd me to leave *Calais*: It was this:

MR. *de Clisson* lodg'd in the same House where I was; as he had never been at the Court of *France*, neither was at that of *Flanders* when I was there, I was not afraid of being known by him. We had several Times convers'd together, and conceiv'd an Esteem for each other. I am come, said he to me, entering my Apartment, and accosting me with

with that Freedom which is ufual among thofe who make Profeffion of Arms; I am come to beg you would be my Second in an Affair which is to be decided this Morning. Honour did not permit me to refufe him, and the Difpofition I was in, made me find a Pleafure in the Thing; I hated all Men, and it was indifferent to me on whom I wreak'd my Revenge.

I MADE Hafte and accouter'd myfelf for the Engagement. We went to the Place of Affignation; our Adverfaries were there before us. The Combat began, and though it was with much Warmth, it was at an End almoft as foon as it began. Our two Enemies were wounded and difarm'd. I afk your Pardon, faid *Cliffon* to me, for having engag'd you to unfheath your Sword againft a Man, with whom there was fo little Credit to be got; but though I could not furnifh your Courage with an Exercife fufficiently noble, I can, if you
will

will follow me, give your Generofity an Employment worthy of it. I affur'd *Cliffon* he might depend upon me.

WITHOUT lofing a Moment's Time we convey'd ourfelves from the Place where we fought ; we crofs'd the Town, and alighted at a Houfe at the other End of the Suburb : Two Women, mafk'd, were waiting for us there. *Cliffon* took one of them and plac'd her before him on his Horfe, and defir'd me to do the like by the other. In the Difpofition I was in, I own if the Bufinefs had been to carry off a Woman, I had not fo eafily have lent a Hand to what was defir'd of me, but now there was no retreating ; we travell'd with all the Diligence we poffibly could. The Wearinefs of our Horfes oblig'd us to ftop towards the Clofe of the Day in a Village, where we luckily met with others, which carried us to *Ypres*. As we were now out of the *French* Terri-tories, our Ladies, who greatly wanted repofe, pafs'd the Night there.

IT

IT was not 'till we got thither that I underſtood what this Adventure was, wherein you ſee I had however ſo great a Share; my own concerns had too much engroſs'd my Thoughts to leave any Room for Curioſity. *Cliſſon* inform'd me, that upon his Return from *England*, whither he had gone with the Counteſs *de Monfort*, he and Mr. *de Mauny* had ſtopt at *Calais*; that they had fallen in Love, he with Mademoiſelle *d'Auxy*, and *Mauny* with Mademoiſelle *de Liancourt*; both under the Power of their Brothers, who had reſolv'd to make a double Match, and in this View they had bred them up together under the Conduct of an old Grandmother of Mademoiſelle *de Liancourt*. Both of them, averſe to the Yoke that was intended to be impos'd upon them, had ſtrengthen'd themſelves in a Reſolution to marry none but whom they could love.

MR. *de Cliſſon* and Mr. *de Mauny* inſpir'd them with ſuch Sentiments as they
choſe to have for their Huſbands. It
was reſolv'd upon among them, that
they ſhould take an Opportunity to get
away from Madam *de Liancourt*'s; that
their Lovers, after being betroth'd to
them, ſhould carry them into *Britany*.
Mauny was oblig'd to go over to *England*, he had ſtrong Reaſons for not declaring his Marriage ; and *Cliſſon* was a-
lone charg'd with the Execution of the
Scheme. The Ladies, having eſcap'd
away by Night, went and ſhelter'd
themſelves at that Houſe in the Suburb,
where they were conceal'd two Days,
when *Cliſſon* and myſelf went to them.

THE two Brothers, being made acquainted with their Flight, doubted not
but *Cliſſon* was the Author of it ; no
Suſpicion fell on Mr. *de Mauny*, who
had been abſent a good While before.
Mr. *d'Auxy* and Mr. *de Liancourt* ſent
Mr.

Mr. *de Cliſſon* a Challenge, being fully perſuaded that the Perſon he would chuſe for his Second could be no other but he that had run away with Mademoiſelle *de Liancourt.* The Fear of the Place's being diſcover'd where theſe Ladies were conceal'd, oblig'd *Cliſſon,* after the Duel, to deſire my Aſſiſtance in conveying them away. I am of Opinion Mr. *de Mauny* has found Means to ſend his Wife over into *England,* or elſe, perhaps, he has not yet the Liberty of declaring his Marriage.

THIS, continu'd Mr. *de Chalons,* is what makes my Caſe look with ſuch an Air of Guilt. My whole Happineſs depends on Mademoiſelle *de Mailly's* being ſet right in this Matter. Every intervening Moment 'till that be done, is loſt to my Love.

MR. *de Canaple* did not defer ſatisfying his Friend. He ſaw Mademoiſelle *de Mailly;* he told her every Thing that

E 2   Mr.

Mr. *de Chalons* had told him. She eagerly liftned to whatever could juftify Mr. *de Chalons*. Alas! faid fhe, if he is innocent, I am yet more to be pitied; but now let us think of nothing but faving him. I tremble for Fear he fhould be difcover'd in the Place where he is; Meafures muft be taken with the King. Your Friend is unfortunate, you love him; may I add to thefe Motives the Intereft of a young Perfon, whom you know only by her Weakneffes? Give not that Name, Madam, anfwered the Count *de Canaple*, to Sentiments which their Conftancy renders refpectable.

THE Intereft of Mr. *de Chalons* required that Mr. *de Vienne*, the Governor of *Calais*, fhould be made acquainted with what had happen'd. Mr. *de Canaple* was forward to undertake a Bufinefs which tended to give him an ufeful Intercourfe with the Father of Madam *de Granfon*. He had heard nothing of her fince his Departure from *Burgun-*
dy

dy, he hop'd to learn some News of her, he should hear her spoken of, he should speak of her himself; all the these little Advantages become confiderable, especially to those who dare not promise themselves greater.

MR. *de Vienne* saw the Count *de Canaple* with Pleasure, he likewise knew Mr. *de Chalons*; the Probity of neither was suspected by him; he gave entire Credit to what Mr. *de Chalons* said concerning his Friend's Innocence. He took upon himself the obtaining of the King the necessary Orders for Mr. *de Chalons*'s Security.

THE Count *de Canaple*, always taken up with his Love, neglected nothing to insinuate himself into the Favour of Mr. *de Vienne*; he paid him great Deference, he render'd him most obsequious Services, he was desirous of being belov'd by any Thing that Madam *de Granson* lov'd; and although he could

E 3   not

not well expect any Return from her, though she might even be still ignorant of it; yet this Occupation sooth'd the Softness of his Heart. It ask'd several Days to bring Mr. *de Vienne* to speak of what he desir'd; for though he had resolv'd to speak of it himself, the Awe, the Fearfulness inseparable from true Love withheld him a long Time.

MR. *de Vienne*, one of the most famous Captains of his Age, did not willingly discourse of any Thing but War. Those who convers'd with him were to undergo the Recital of many a Battle before they were privileg'd to put Questions. At last, Mr. *de Canaple*, embolden'd by the Familiarity he had acquir'd, ventur'd to ask News concerning Madam *de Granson*. She is, answer'd Mr. *de Vienne*, in the Country, and has been ever since her Husband's Departure. At *Vermanton*, I suppose? said Mr. *de Canaple*. No; reply'd Mr. *de Vienne*, she has taken a Dislike to that

that Place, and will go there no more; nay, she's going to part with it.

MR. *de Canaple*, instructed by his Love, saw into the Cause of this Dislike, and it pain'd him to the Heart. However, as that Place infinitely affected him, though in afflicting him, he was resolved to be the Owner of it. An Agent of his was immediately dispatch'd away into *Burgundy*, with Orders to purchase *Vermanton*, cost what it would. The Buying of the Goods was expresly and in a more especial Manner enjoin'd; every Thiug that had belonged to Madam *de Granson*, and which she had made Use of, were of infinite Value to the Count *de Canaple*; even that Bed wherein he had been so blest, was not exempted. Love, when it is extreme, admits of no Preference.

HEARTS that are sensible presently divine each others Thoughts. Madam *de Granson* saw into the Motives of the

E 4   Count

Count *de Canaple*'s offering an exceſſive
Price for *Vermanton* ; ſhe was even of
Opinion that he liked this Place for the
very Reaſon which ſhe had for diſliking
it ; and therefore ſhe obſtructed his Buying it.   The Count *de Canaple* look'd
upon this Refuſal as a freſh Inſtance of
her hatred to him.

WHAT Mr. *de Vienne* told him concerning the Privacy wherewith his
Daughter liv'd, ever ſince her Huſband's
Departure, confirm'd him in this Opinion.   The Unfortunate always turn
their Thoughts on that Side which may
encreaſe their Pain.   He perſwaded himſelf that Madam *de Granſon* lov'd her
Huſband more than ever.   'Tis I who
have taught her to love him, ſaid he ;
his Heart has been inſtructed by mine in
all the Delicacies of Love ; my Paſſion
ſerves him for a Model ; ſhe does for her
Huſband what ſhe is ſenſible I would do
for her ; and I have the ſingular hard Fate
that the moſt tender Sentiments which
                                          Love

Love has infpir'd me with, turns folely to the Advantage of my Rival.

THESE diftracting Reflections threw the Count *de Canaple* into a Melancholy, which did not efcape Mademoifelle's ~~Notice~~; *de in it is* fhe faw plainly he was in Love, but without telling him fo. She was thereby the more difpos'd to entertain a Friendfhip for him, and to give him her Confidence. It was likewife a Relief to Mr. *de Canaple* to converfe with one who had a fufceptible Soul, and who, as well as himfelf, experienc'd the Diftreffes of Love.

MEAN while Mr. *de Chalons* recovered of his Wounds; he had quitted his Bed, and prefs'd his Friend, every Time he faw him, to obtain of Mademoifelle *de Mailly* the Favour of fpeaking with her. It is only through her, faid he to him, that I mean to clear up this ftrange Adventure; I know her Franknefs and Veracity: Since fhe ftill loves me, fhe

E 5   will

will have lefs Reluctance to own herfelf guilty, than fhe would have to deceive me.

WHAT is it you afk of me? faid Mademoifelle *de Mailly* to the Count *de Canaple*, when he made the Requeft to her which he was charg'd with. Can I fee the Man, who has fill'd my Father's Houfe with Mourning? This Obftacle, which is itfelf too ftrong, is not the only one which feparates us for ever. I have believ'd him falfe, let him endeavour to become fo; the Intereft of his Repofe requires it, and, if I know the Frame of my own Heart aright, it will be a Confolation to me to think, that at leaft he will not be unhappy, What a ftrange Command is this you lay upon me? faid Mr. *de Canaple*. Confider, that this would be to give Death to my Friend.

DOUBT not I am as much to be pitied, and perhaps more than he, reply'd Mademoifelle

demoiselle *de Mailly*; tell him, if it must
be so, that I no longer deserve his Love.
Can this possibly bring him any Consolation? No, I can't think it: I know,
at least, that my heart was never more
cruelly torn than when I thought him
guilty. But, reply'd Mr. *de Canaple*,
will you not unfold to me the Motives
of a Conduct, which it so much concerns Mr. *de Chalons* to know? He
would be ne'er the less unhappy for that,
reply'd she, and I should say that which
I ought not to say. Let it suffice him
that Fortune only has caus'd his Unhappiness, and mine too; that I could hardly forbear loving him at the very Time
when I believ'd I could no more esteem
him. Would to GOD, said she, fetch-
ing a deep Sigh, I had always believ'd
he lov'd me! If I may yet ask any
Thing of him, I desire he would remove himself from a Place, where his
Presence does nothing but increase my
Sufferings.

E 6 NOTWITH-

NOTWITHSTANDING Mr. *de Cha-lons*'s Respect for Mademoiselle *de Mail-ly*, he could not have submitted to her Orders, had not his Honour and Duty oblig'd him to obey those which he receiv'd from the King.   Mr. *de Canaple* and he were sent for, to *Paris*, to deliberate on the approaching Campaign.

MADAM *de Granson* had been arriv'd there some Days, to attend her Husband who was dangerously sick ; he could gladly have dispens'd with so much Solicitude. His Heart had not been idle amidst a Court which breathed Gallantry ; the fine Women, who compos'd it, had a Share, one after another, in his Homages. Madam *de Montmorency* was the last to whom he had devoted himself, and his Passion for her was not over when he fell sick.

MADAM *de Granson* did not at first perceive the Indifference with which her

tender

tender Cares were repaid; or if she did
perceive it, she imputed it to the Condition Mr. *de Granson* was in. But as this
Indifference increas'd, she saw what she
had not at first seen; and it was a Sort
of Consolation to her; she fancy'd she
was thereby become less culpable in Regard to him. Being freed from the
Necessity which she had impos'd on herself to love him, she behav'd herself to
him in a freer and more natural Manner
than before.

She had taken no Precaution for the
avoiding Mr. *de Canaple*, whom she believ'd to be at a great Distance from *Paris*. He found her in Mr. *de Granson*'s
Chamber when he came thither. The
Surprise and Confusion they were both
in, were extremely great. Mr. *de Granson* too had his Share therein; he was
naturally of a weak Cast of Mind, always such as the Persons he convers'd
with were minded to have him be. The
Presence of Mr. *de Canaple*, whose Virtue

tue he well knew, tacitly upbraided him
with his Conduct; he fear'd his Auste-
rity: He fain would have gone on in
the Way of Life he then led.

AFTER some general Discourse, these
three Persons, not knowing what to say,
kept Silence. Madam *de Granson*, ad-
monish'd that she ought to shun the
Count *de Canaple*, by the small Repugnance she had to see him, was for going out; but Mr. *de Granson* stopt her.
As he was the freest Person of the three,
he began to ask his Friend some Questions concerning Mr. *de Vienne*. How
much soever Madam *de Granson* was concerned in this Conversation, the Fear
of directing her Speech to Mr. *de Canaple*, hinder'd her from taking a Part
in it. But Mr. *de Vienne* having writ
to his Daughter and Mr. *de Granson* a
great many very advantageous Things
in Relation to the Count *de Canaple*;
Mr. *de Granson* was eager to tell them
him, and appeal'd to his Wife as a
                              Voucher

Voucher thereof. It is true, said she casting her Eyes to the Ground.

A MOMENT afterwards, Mr. *de Granson* having some Orders to give one of his Servants, Madam *de Granson* found herself oblig'd to say something to Mr. *de Canaple* that she might not give him the least Room for talking of Mr. *de Vienne*; so she put him upon speaking of the Ladies of *Calais*. I have seen nothing, Madam, said he to her timorously and without daring to look on her, but the Father . . . . he would have said of Madam *de Granson*, but he stopt short; and recollecting himself again after some Moments silence, I have seen nothing but Mr. *de Vienne*.

NONE of these Marks of Tenderness escap'd the Observation of Mademoiselle *de Granson*; in Despight of herself the *culpable* disappear'd, and left her nothing to see but the *amiable* and the *enamour'd*. In Proportion to the
Increase

Increase of this Impression upon her, she
was the more studious to shun him ; but
the Necessity of being in her Husband's
Chamber, and the Privilege Mr. *de Canaple* had of coming thither at all Hours,
put it out of her Power to avoid him :
It is true he used this Privilege with so
much Discretion that Madam *de Granson*
became used to see him, and was imperceptibly reconcil'd thereto.

HER Husband's Inconcern towards
her, now made a very different Impression on her Mind ; she could not forbear, since Mr. *de Canaple* was a Witness of it, to feel it and to be offended
at it. This Sentiment, of which she
was not long in discovering the Cause,
inspir'd her with Indignation against herself ; but, notwithstanding all the Severity of her Reflections, she was not able,
for some Days after, to get the better
of her Sensibility.

MR.

MR. *de Granson*, when he departed
from Home, had afk'd her, not having
had Time to get her Picture drawn, for
a Bracelet of great Value, wherein was
that of the late Madam *de Vienne*, whom
her Daughter fo perfectly refembled that
it feem'd as if fhe had fat for it herfelf.
She had taken it off her Bracelet with
much Regret, and had defir'd Mr. *de
Granson* to keep it very carefully. As
the Converfation was not over brifk
between Hufband and Wife, and that
Mr. *de Canaple's* Prefence ftill laid it under greater Reftraints ; Madam *de Granson*, for Want of other Difcourfe, afk'd
Mr. *de Granson* for that Picture. He
was fo confus'd at this Requeft, and fo
little Mafter of his Confufion, that
Madam *de Granson* found he had parted
with it: She was in no wife prepar'd to
fupport fuch a Kind of Contempt. Some
Tears ftole down her Cheeks, and to
conceal them fhe left the Room. But
this Care was in vain, Mr. *de Canaple*
took

took Notice of them ; and though what he saw was not likely to leſſen his Jea-louſy, but rather added to it, yet a tender Concern for the Misfortune of one he loved, and the Indignation which he conceived againſt Mr. *de Granſon*, put to Silence every other Sentiment.

MAY I believe what I ſee ? ſaid he to him as ſoon as they were alone. How ! have you no Love, nor even common Reſpect for your Wife ? for a Wife, who deſerves the Reſpect and Adora-tion of the whole Earth ? She pours forth Tears ; you make her unhappy ; and where have you found Charms pow-erful enough to efface the Impreſſion which hers had made on your Heart ?

WHAT would you have ? replied Mr. *de Granſon* ; it is none of my Fault : After all, where do you find, that a Man ought always to be fond of his Wife ? This is ſo odd a Fancy, ſo un-

common

common a Way of Thinking, that,
were I guilty of it, I fhould hide it from
you. I will likewife own to you, the
Fondnefs of my Wife, of which I receive every Day new Inftances, perplexes
me, but does not touch me.

MR. *de Canaple*, who was before fo
tenderly concerned on Madam *de Granfon*'s Account, at this Word Fondnefs,
felt all his Jealoufy awake. The Refentment with which he was ftung, made
him wifh that Mr. *de Granfon* was yet
more culpable. He was no longer able
to difapprove his Conduct, and went
from him, more incenfed againft Madam
de Granfon, than he had been againft
him.

SHE is then fond? faid he. If my
Love could not move her, it might at
leaft have taught her the Value fhe was
of, and have faved her from the Weaknefs and the Shame of loving one who
loves not her. I could pardon her, nay
I could

I could admire her, if her Procedure was dictated only by Duty; but she loves, she is jealous; and whilst I mind nothing but her, she minds nothing but the Loss of a Heart which is far less valuable than mine.... Alas! her Virtue has given Rise to her Tenderness; she is unhappy as well as myself, with this Difference, that I am only so for having admitted into my Heart a Passion which so many Reasons engaged me to oppose. I cannot be beloved; I must create to myself another kind of Happiness; I must speak to her Husband; I must bring him back to her again: She must, if it is possible, be beholden to me for the Happiness which she shall enjoy.

As Madam *de Granson* seemed much concerned for the Loss of her Bracelet, Mr. *de Canaple* used his utmost Endeavours to recover it; and succeeded. The Resemblance of the Picture was a furious Temptation to keep it; but this Pleasure would not have been comparable to

that

that of giving Madam *de Granſon* ſo ſenſible a Proof of his Diligence to pleaſe her, and a Satisfaction which ſhe would owe to him alone: He even hoped, ſhe would apprehend it to be the Effect of Reſpectfulneſs, his not preſuming to keep what ſhe would not chooſe to have given him.

NOTWITHSTANDING the Liberty which Mr. *de Canaple* enjoyed at Mr. *de Granſon's*, there were certain Hours ſince his Illneſs, when none but his Domeſtics were permitted to come into his Chamber. Mr. *de Canaple*, that he might have a Pretext for going into Madam *de Granſon's* Apartment, pitched upon one of theſe Hours. Emboldened by the Action he was going to do, his Mien and his Countenance were leſs timorous   Madam *de Granſon* took Offence at it, and gave him a Look which diſcovered to him what paſſed within her Breaſt. It is to reſtore you, Madam, ſaid he to her, the Picture, the Loſs whereof

whereof seemed to have troubled you,
that I have presumed so far as to enter
your Apartment. I never could comprehend, pursued he in presenting it to
her, how it was possible for Mr. *de
Granson* to part with a Thing which
ought to have been so precious to him,
and I comprehend it still less at this Moment.

THESE last Words were delivered in
a low and softening Tone. Madam *de
Granson*, astonished, and softening likewise herself at Mr. *de Canaple's* Procedure, knew not what Course to take.
It was doing him a Favour, to receive
this Mark of his Devotedness; and if
she refused it him, she left her Picture
in his Hands. She chose the gentlest
Method. Her Heart played her false,
without her perceiving it. However,
being still equally studious to fulfil her
Duty with the utmost Exactness; I
could have wished, Sir, said she to him
taking the Picture, that you had pleased

to

to have given it to Mr. *de Granſon* ; but I will not let him remain ignorant of this freſh Inſtance of your Friendſhip. To put an end to a Converſation which embaraſs'd her, ſhe roſe up, in order to go into Mr. *de Granſon*'s Room, and Mr. *de Canaple* did not preſume to follow her thither.

MADAM *de Granſon* accordingly went into her Huſband's Room, to inform him of what had happened ; but when ſhe was to ſpeak, ſhe found herſelf at a loſs. It came into her Mind, that it was deceiving Mr. *de Granſon*, and deceiving him in the moſt unworthy Manner, to engage him to any Acknowledgment to Mr. *de Canaple*. This Notion, ſo capable of alarming her Virtue, determined her to Silence.

As faſt as Mr. *de Granſon* recovered his Health, his Friends re-aſſembled themſelves at his Houſe. Madam *de Granſon* appeared but little, and always

in

in an Undress; but at length she shewed herself, and it was impossible for her Beauty not to make an Impression. Mr. *de Chatillon*, though engaged by the Character he had gained in the World, not to be in Love, could not help being touched with Madam *de Granson*'s Charms, more seriously than was necessary for his Repose. His natural Presumption did not let him foresee any bad Consequence from it; he only wanted an Opportunity to declare himself; it had been difficult to find one, if Mr. *de Granson*, who above all things feared to be suspected of being fond or jealous of his Wife, had not obliged her to continue with him at a Time when there was the most Company.

THOUGH Galantry, and especially Love, seemed to the young Fellows of the Court a sort of a Jest, the Presence of Madam *de Granson* gave a galant Turn to all Conversation: She herself
took

took no Share therein. Mr. *de Canaple* condemned himfelf before her to the fame Silence; and when fhe was not there, the Fear of being gueffed at engaged him to be much upon the Referve. But all thefe Confiderations forfook him in the Heat of a Difpute, which turned upon the Pleafures of Gallantry and thofe of Love. He could not endure they fhould be compared together; and, not remembering that he acted in the World the Part of an *Indifferent*, he fell to drawing the moft lively and the moft animated Picture that could be of two Perfons who loved each other, and concluded with averring, not without Vehemence, That the Favours of the fineft Woman in the World would never touch him, if he did not poffefs her Heart.

HEYDAY! cried Mr. *de Granfon*; whereabouts are we now? How long has Mr. *de Canaple* been fo well acquainted with all thefe Niceties? Would

F   you

you think it, Madam, said he to Madam *de Granson*, who was coming in that Moment, this *Canaple*, so averse to Love, is become its most zealous Advocate! He is for no Galantry, he is all for pure downright Passion; and, from his Way of Talking, on my Conscience, I believe the Man is in Love.

THE Sight of Madam *de Granson* immediately made the Count *de Canaple* silent; and instead of answering, he reproached himself for saying what he did, as an Act of Indiscretion. His Confusion had doubtless been taken notice of, if Mr. *de Chalons*, who was also present, had not begun to speak. I am of the same Opinion, said he, with Mr. *de Canaple*; the Pleasure of Loving is the greatest Happiness; and perhaps we should be less sensible of the Unhappiness of being betrayed, were it not for the Necessity we find ourselves then in of renouncing so delightful a State. But, replied Mr. *Montmorency* laughing,

why

why should you commit this Violence on yourself? You may love your fill, and be as fond as you please of a Mistress who shall have broke her Faith with you, nobody will be your Hindrance; and I dare say, your Felicity will be neither interrupted nor envied.

You may laugh as much as you please, said Mr. *de Chalons*; but I would freely forgive, provided I found in the Sincerity of Repentance, and in an undisguised frank Confession, Matter enough to persuade me I was beloved, even at the Time I was betrayed. There is, methinks, a kind of Sweetness in forgiving what one loves; it is acquiring an additional Right of being beloved, and one loves one's self the more for it.

With such Maxims as these, you are far from being jealous, said Mr. *de Granson*. At least I am very differently so from most Men, replied he, who

F 2   know

know not this Sentiment otherwise than by an inordinate Self-love. Mine does not quarrel with the Infidelities that may be practised towards me, they only afflict my Heart.

I CONFESS, said Mr. *de Chatillon*, interrupting, and who had not hitherto spoke at all, I do not understand these Distinctions of Love and Self-love ; I only know, that the Women will always prefer a Lover whose Jealousy shall be full of Rage, before all your Respectfulness and all your Delicacies.

COULD you forgive, Madam, said he to Madam *de Granson* approaching to her Ear, a Man who should be afraid of losing your Heart, and yet preserve his Reason ? Nobody, answered she aloud with a haughty and scornful Tone, shall have it in their Power to suffer such a Loss ; and without looking on him, without giving him Time to answer, she got up to go away.

THOUGH

THOUGH Mr. *de Canaple* durſt not caſt his Eyes on her, his Attentiveneſs and Application ſupplied his Eyes. He perceived Mr. *de Chatillon*'s Paſſion almoſt as ſoon as himſelf. A Man of this Character was no dangerous Rival with Madam *de Granſon*. But a Rival, tho' ever ſo little to be feared, is always troubleſome. Madam *de Granſon*'s Anſwer, and the Tone of Voice with which ſhe made it, recompenſed him for the Pain he had ſuffered in ſeeing Mr. *de Chatillon* ſo bold as to whiſper her. A Lover, and eſpecially an unfortunate Lover, takes as a Favour done to himſelf the Severities that are exerciſed on his Rivals.

MR. *de Chatillon* was not a Man to be diſcouraged at this Shock. He followed Madam *de Granſon*, in hopes of giving her his Hand. Mr. *de Canaple*, who now had nothing to ſtay him, left the Company likewiſe. They were both

near

near Madam *de Granson*'s Chariot, when she was going to step into it. Mr. *de Canaple* however did not dare to offer her his Hand ; but Mr. *de Chatillon* shewed no such Awe : Madam *de Granson*, provoked at his Boldness, and resolving to repress it, took that of Mr. *de Canaple* ; and did not perceive how soothing this Preference was to him, but by feeling that Hand tremble. So she hastily quitted it, and got into her Chariot.

THIS was the first Moment Mr. *de Canaple* had found any Ease. He would fain have been alone and enjoyed it at leisure ; but Mr. *de Chalons* coming up to him that Instant, deprived him of the Liberty of doing it. How happy are you ! said he to him ; for notwithstanding the Suspicions you have given occasion for to-day, I am persuaded you are in love with nobody. As for me, I am the Victim of a Passion which promises me nothing but Torments, and which

which I have not even the Resolution to combat.

MR. *de Canaple* could not tell how to own he was in Love, neither could he resolve to disown it ; this had been a doing Wrong either to his Love or his Discretion. Let us not talk of Me, answered he, I am what I can, and I would not advise any one to envy my Condition.

MR. *de Chalons*, full of his own Impressions, did not concern himself to penetrate into those of his Friend. I have been more upon the Rack to-day than I have ever been, said he to him ; the Picture which I have been making of my Passion, has awakened it to a greater Degree, and engraved it more deeply in my Heart. For Heaven's Sake, write to Mademoiselle *de Mailly* : It is a Liberty I am not allowed ; but it will be almost receiving a Letter from Me, the receiving One from You.

I shall

I shall employ her Thoughts at least a Moment or two ; and what a Satisfaction is not that to me !

THE Count *de Canaple* was in the proper Disposition for the well-expressing of his Friend's Sentiments. But this Friend was too much enamoured to be easily contented. The Letter was made up, and opened again, more than once ; and at last delivered to a Domestick of Mr. *de Canaple*'s, who was ordered to carry it to *Calais*, and bring back an Answer.

IN the Interim the Departure of the King was fixed, and all such as were not particularly attached to his Person, were desirous to go before, and accordingly prepared to set forwards. Mr. *de Canaple* was of this Number : The Difficulty of removing from what one loves, is not to an unhappy Lover the same as to a Lover beloved.

WHEN

WHEN Mr. *de Granson*'s Health permitted him to go abroad, he had a Mind Madam *de Granson* fhould be prefented to the King and the two Queens; her Beauty was admired by every body. The Praifes which were lavifhed on her, increafed Mr. *de Chatillon*'s Ardour. He followed her wherever fhe went; in fpite of the Mode and the Strain which he had contracted from the fafhionable World, he made Love to her in plain Terms. Madam *de Granson*, quite angry at his Importunities, and vexed at herfelf and at Love, took Revenge by the Rigours fhe exercifed on Him, for what Herfelf felt for his Rival; this Rival was oftentimes a Witnefs of it, and though He was treated with yet greater Severity, it was at leaft not accompanied with that Scorn and Contempt with which Mr. *de Chatillon* was loaded. Madam *de Granson* could no way avoid the Compliment of their Adieus. Mr. *de Chatillon* had ftill the

Boldnefs

Boldneſs to talk the ſame Language ;
Mr. *de Canaple*, on the contrary, pronounced not a ſingle Word.

THIS Difference of Behaviour was
but too much taken Notice of by Madam *de Granſon*. The Upbraiding which
ſhe inceſſantly made againſt herſelf,
turned out to the Advantage of her
Duty ; ſhe ſtill believed ſhe did not
ſufficiently well acquit herſelf. Inſtead
of being diſcouraged at the little Regard
ſhewn her by Mr. *de Granſon*, ſhe redoubled her Services and her Attention
to him.

As he was to attend on the King,
he ſet not out ſo ſoon as Mr. *de Canaple*.
Madam *de Granſon* perceived that her
Preſence was a Conſtraint to him. But
without expoſtulating with him, without ſhewing the leaſt Diſcontent, ſhe
diſpoſed herſelf to go to *Calais*, that
ſhe might the more expeditiouſly have
News from the Army, and be with a
Father

Father whom she loved, and by whom she was tenderly beloved. This was, in the present Frame and Posture of her Heart, a Consolation, and an Occasion of being able to give herself up to Sentiments of a warrantable Friendship.

MR. *de Vienne* received his Daughter with Joy; she was visited by all the most considerable People of the Town. Mademoiselle *de Mailly* was not among the last that paid this kind of Duty; they had both of them those Qualities which set so favourable a Bias on Peoples Minds, and give Birth to an Inclination. Accordingly the very first Moment of their Acquaintance they found themselves in the same Freedom, as if they had known each other of a long time. Madam *de Granson*, charmed with Mademoiselle *de Mailly*'s Wit and agreeable Person, often spoke of her to Mr. *de Vienne*.

F 6 Ι WOULD

I WOULD gladly, said she to him, spend my Days with so delightful a young Lady; but I am ready to die with Fear, left she should soon be snatched from us by some great Match. On the contrary, replied Mr. *de Vienne*, Marriage may bring her nearer to you. *Canaple*, adds he, in the Stay he made here, seemed to have a more than ordinary Respect for her. He is come hither again, upon no other Account but to see Her. And it is not long since they brought a Man to me who had a Letter for her, who would not at first tell his Name, but was forced to own he belonged to the Count *de Canaple*. For a Man of his Temper, so much Affiduity proves a great deal. Madam *de Granfon* felt at this Discourse a Disorder and Emotion she had hitherto been a Stranger to. She had not Power to continue the Conversation any longer, when Mademoiselle *de Mailly* came in.

MR.

MR. *de Vienne*, who was rather a Plain-dealer than a polite Man, was not afraid of putting her out of Countenance, by repeating what he had juſt ſaid to his Daughter. Mademoiſelle *de Mailly* could not hear without bluſhing, a Name which was linked in her Imagination with that of her Lover. But as People cannot well forbear talking of Things which they have at Heart, eſpecially if they can do it with Innocence ; Mademoiſelle *de Mailly*, after ſhe had ſlightly ſaid that Mr. *de Canaple* was no Lover of her's, indulged herſelf the Pleaſure of praiſing him for Qualities which he had in common with Mr. *de Chalons*, and praiſed him with Warmth.

MADAM *de Granſon* had beheld him till then with the ſame Eyes, and even more favourably. But as he appeared ſuch to Mademoiſelle *de Mailly*, he now ceaſed to appear ſo to her. Over-ruled by a Senſation which ſhe was unacquainted with,

with, she could not refrain from contra-
dicting what was said. Mr. *de Vienne*,
who thought his Daughter unjust, took
Sides against her. Mademoiselle *de
Mailly*, strengthen'd by Mr. *de Vienne's*
Authority, presently maintain'd her O-
pinion with a Warmth very improper
to bring over Madam *de Granson*; but
as the latter was in Possession of a greater Tranquillity of Mind, she hasten'd to
finish the Dispute.

MADAM *de Granson*, being left alone,
was seiz'd with a more violent and more
tormenting Pain than she had hitherto
experienc'd. The Reflexions which she
had made on what had pass'd, gave her
such Suspicion, and even Certainty, as
quite overcame her. I cannot doubt it,
said she, he is in Love, he is belov'd.
What I have now seen can only be inspir'd by Love, and a contented Love too.

WHAT! whilst I stood in Need of
my Virtue to remember the Injury he
did me, whilst I thought him solely taken

ken up in repairing it, whilft the Appearances of his Refpect made fo fhame-
ful an Impreffion on my Heart, does he
place his Love elfewhere? How have I
been able to deceive myfelf? How have
I been able to give fo forc'd an Interpretation to his Proceedings? How have
I been been able to believe that a Man
in Love could be always fo much Mafter of himfelf? No, no; he would
have fpoke to me, at the Hazard of
difpleafing me.

SHE afterwards called to Mind, that,
in the Converfation where the Count *de
Canaple* maintain'd the Part of Love,
he was filent as foon as fhe appear'd.
His Nicenefs would have been offended,
faid fhe, to fpeak of Love before any
other Woman but his Miftrefs. How
do I know whether he did not think
he ought to be cautious on my Account? Who can affure me he did not
fufpect my Weaknefs? This Thought
forc'd Tears from Madam *de Granfon*;
and

and as she now discovered nothing in the
Count *de Canaple*'s Conduct which could
plead in his Favour, her whole Resentment was awaken'd. It would hardly
have kept itself up amidst the Praises
which were daily shower'd down on Mr.
de Canaple's Valour, and at a Time
when his Life was expos'd to so many
and such imminent Dangers: But Mademoiselle *de Mailly*, who saw, in the
Perils which attended Mr. *de Canaple*,
those of Mr. *de Chalons*, seem'd so much
affected thereby, that Madam *de Granson*
ceas'd to be so.

COLDNESS, nay Aversion had succeeded in her Heart to the Kindness she
had at first felt for her. Chance had
again brought them together, when
Tidings came that the Army was
marching to the Enemy and that Mr,
de Canaple's Troop and that of Mr. *de
Chalons* were to begin the Attack.
Mademoiselle *de Mailly*, struck with
this News, was unable to conceal her
Trouble

Trouble. Madam *de Granfon* was in no calmer a Condition. Mr. *de Vienne* imputed the Diforder of her Mind to the Fear fhe was in on Mr. *de Granfon*'s Account, and finifh'd her Depreffion by the Pains he took to raife her Spirits, and by the Praife which he ceas'd not to beftow on the Greatnefs of her Affection. What would my Father think? faid fhe; what would all about me think, were the Depth of my Heart known, were they appriz'd that the Tears he commends proceed but from my Weaknefs? It is at leaft neceffary that the Knowlege I have of it fhould recal my Virtue, and that I free myfelf from the cruel Torture of being to myfelf an Object of Contempt.

THE Lofs of the Battle of * *Creffy*, of which Advice was then brought, and

---

* *Auguft* 26, 1346, was fought the Battle of *Creffy*, in the Reign of *Philip of Valois*, wherein upwards of Thirty Thoufand common Soldiers, and

the

the dangerous Wounds which Mr. *de Granson* had receiv'd in it, gave Madam *de Granson*'s Virtue a new Exercise. She did not hesitate a Moment on the Course she had to take; and without being stopt by Mr. *de Vienne*'s Intreaties, or the Dangers she expos'd herself to in crossing a Country full of Soldiers, she immediately set out. Her Father not being able to retain her, gave her a strong and numerous Guard. They were attack'd, at different Times, by Parties of the Enemy, whom they repuls'd with Success. The Idea of Mr. *de Canaple* often presented itself to Madam *de Granson* in her Passage. The Uncertainty she was in as to what had been his Fate, of which she had not Resolution enough to make Inquiry, les-

a prodigious Number of *French* Lords and Gentlemen perish'd by the Arms of the *English*, who made use of Cannon, the first that had been seen 'till then. *From the Abbé Valerot's Journal de la France, dedicated to the present King of France.*

sen'd

fen'd her Anger, and difpos'd her to have more of Pity than Refentment.

THE Third Day of her Journey, her little Troop, which had been weaken'd by the preceding Combats, was attack'd by fome *Englifh* Troopers, very much fuperior in Number. Madam *de Granfon* was upon the Point of falling into the Conqueror's Hands, had not a Cavalier, who was going to *Calais*, come to her Relief; he faw the Combat at a Diftance, and though he was accompany'd by very few, he made no Delay to attack the *Englifh*. The *French* who had been put to the Rout, took Courage again, rally'd themfelves to him, and affifted him in refcuing Madam *de Granfon*'s Chariot from the Hands of thofe who had, by this Time, feiz'd it.

THE Trouble fhe was in had-not permitted her to diftinguifh what was doing, and taking her Deliverers for her
Enemy

Enemy, when he came to her Chariot, if you are a Gentleman, said she to him with a Voice which Fear had almost entirely chang'd, but which could never be undiscoverable by him to whom she spoke, you will put me to a Ransom without Delay. How! cry'd he out without giving her Time to say another Word, is it Madam *de Granson!* and does she take me for an Enemy! No, Madam, you have none here, said he to her; all those about you are ready to sacrifice their Lives to defend you, and to obey you.

MADAM *de Granson*'s Pride and a certain Magnanimity of Spirit which was natural to her, had given her Strength in the Beginning of this Adventure; but Mr. *de Canaple*'s Voice threw her into a Condition far more hard to support than that out of which she was just come; a Thousand different Thoughts crowded into her Mind. This Man who had so highly offended her, whom she

she must hate to save herself from the Shame of Loving, has just now expos'd his Life for her ; and this same Man was going to *Calais*, doubtless to see Mademoiselle *de Mailly*.

ACKNOWLEDGEMENT of the Service could not subsist with this Reflexion, and left in the Soul of Madam *de Granson* nothing but the Chagrin and Displeasure of having receiv'd it. Mr. *de Canaple* was waiting for the Orders she would be pleas'd to give him, and would have waited much longer had not Mr. *de Vienne*'s Gentleman of the Horse, who led the Escorte, come and press'd him to a Conclusion. She was for prosecuting her Purpose, but would not have Mr. *de Canaple* to accompany her ; the secret Resentment with which she was animated, did not allow her to receive from him a Service which she could no longer place to the Account of Chance.

YOUR

YOUR Generosity has done enough, Sir, said she to him, haste away to *Calais*, where, I apprehend, you have a very important Call. It is true, Madam, said the Count *de Canaple*, I have Orders to repair to *Calais* ; but however express they are I cannot execute them 'till you are in a Place where you will have nothing further to fear.

MADAM *de Granson*, not being able to do better, committed herself to his Care. The desperate Condition wherein she found Mr. *de Granson* at her Arrival at *Amiens*, excus'd her from returning her Thanks to Mr. *de Canaple*, who immediately resum'd the Road to *Calais*.

MR. *de Granson* had passionately lov'd his Wife; what she did for him at a Time so near that wherein he had been false to her, the Thought that Death was going to part them, awaken'd his Tenderness, and stretching out his Hand

to

4

to her as soon as he saw her, I am not worthy of you, said he to her; Heaven punishes me for not having known the Blessing I possess'd; I am sincerely sorry for the Wrongs I have been guilty of; forgive me them, and never remember them but as that Remembrance may be necessary to your Consolation.

MADAM *de Granson* bedew'd with her Tears the Hand which her Husband had presented to her; the Repentance which he express'd to her pierc'd her with Shame and Grief; she thought herself alone culpable, she condemn'd herself for not having lov'd Mr. *de Granson*; and the Error she was in on that Account seem'd to her a Sort of Treachery. I have nothing to pardon you for, said she to him still pouring forth a Flood of Tears, I would give my own Life to preserve yours. Mr. *de Granson* would have answer'd her, but his Strength forsook him; he was a long Time in a Kind of fainting Fit,

out

out of which he recover'd indeed, but knew nobody, and died two Days after Madam *de Granson*'s Arrival.

THIS Spectacle, always fo moving, was yet more fo with Regard to her, on Account of the Circumftances which had attended it. As nobody knew the Danger which threatned *Calais*, fhe return'd thither; being perfuaded that nothing in the World could claim her Concern but Mr. *de Vienne*.

MR. *de Canaple*, at his Arrival, had given Mr. *de Vienne* no Manner of Hopes of Mr. *de Granson*'s Life. The public Calamity, faid this great Captain, does not let me feel my private Misfortunes; but how is it poffible that an Army, compos'd of all the Gentry and moft of the Nobility of *France*, that is to fay, of all that is moft brave in the Univerfe, fhould be beaten?

IN

IN order to conquer, said Mr. *de Ca-*
naple, more Prudence was neceffary and
lefs of Courage; this Nobility and Gentry
which you fpeak of, rely'd too much on
their Valour, and defpis'd Precautions.
The King, after he was gone from *Ab-*
beville where he was encamp'd, detach'd
fome Troops under the Conduct of
Meffieurs *des Noyers, de Beaujeux, d'Au-*
bigny, and *des Dromefnil,* to go and view
the *Englifh.* At their Return, *Dromef-*
nil, embolden'd by a clear and unfpotted
Reputation and by an Intrepidity of
Courage which he was confcious of in
himfelf, had alone the Refolution to
tell the King he ought not to attack the
Enemy.

ALTHOUGH the Army was, before
this, on their March; the King, con-
vinc'd by the Reafons of this gallant
Man, fent Orders to the *Genoefe,* who
compos'd the Van, to make an Halt.
Whether they had been corrupted, as

G   is

is fuſpected, or were afraid of loſing their Rank, they refuſed to obey; the ſecond Column, ſeeing the March of the firſt, continu'd their March too. The Battle was join'd, and the Generals were oblig'd to follow the Impetuoſity of their Troops.

THEY never diſcover'd more Ardency; but we fought without any Manner of Order, on a Ground which was diſadvantageous to Us, and againſt an Army that was not only more numerous, but wherein Diſcipline too was ſtrictly obſerv'd. Notwithſtanding theſe Advantages, the Troop which I commanded had ſurrounded the Prince of *Wales**. This young Prince, to whom *Edward* had refus'd the Succour which he had ſent to aſk of him, having no-

---

* The King of *England*, when he was deſir'd to ſend a Reinforcement to the Prince of *Wales*, anſwer'd, *Let the Boy win his Spurs*; reſolving with himſelf that the Prince ſhould have the ſole Honour of that Day's Victory.

thing

thing to depend on but his Courage, acted Wonders. His Men, animated by his Example, redoubled their Efforts, and he got out of our Hands. I saw myself abandon'd by my Men, and if the Night had not favour'd my Retreat, I had been kill'd or taken Prisoner. I had likewise the good Fortune to disengage poor *Granson* from a Troop of Soldiers, by whom he was inclos'd; I conducted him to *Amiens*. The King, who retired thither, ordered me to come hither, to see the Condition of the Place, and to consult with you about the Means to preserve it.

A MAN who was sent by Mademoiselle *de Mailly* to Mr. *de Canaple* to desire she might see him a Moment, did not give Mr. *de Vienne* an Opportunity to answer him: He follow'd the Man who had been sent to him, and promis'd Mr. *de Vienne* to return again presently.

MADE-

MADEMOISELLE *de Mailly*, as foon as fhe had heard his Voice, rofe up haftily to go and meet him; but the Agitations of her Heart and Pain of Mind were fo violent that fhe found it not poffible for her to ftir one Step from her Chair; fo fuffering herfelf to be carried to him as fhe fat; Ah! Sir, faid fhe as foon as fhe faw Mr. *de Canaple*, fay nothing to me, I am ready to die with Uncertainty, and yet have not the Power to get out of it. I do affure you, faid he to her, I have no fuch dreadful News to tell you. Is it poffible, cry'd fhe again with a Sort of Tranfport, that I fhould be fo happy! What! can he be fafe? And where is he? Is he not wounded? I cannot anfwer you pofitively, reply'd Mr. *de Canaple*, I know he is not in the Number of the Dead, and is but a Prifoner at worft. Ah! faid fhe, he would never yield but in the utmoft Extremity; if he is a Prifoner, I behold him cover'd with
Wounds:

Wounds: Alas! it is I who have added Defpair to his natural Bravery. He was carelefs of a Life which I have made unhappy.

THE Abundance of Tears which fhe fhed, the repeated Sighings which cut off her Speech, put a Stop to her Laments, and gave the Count *de Canaple* Time to remove her Fears and encourage her a little. He promis'd her, in taking his Leave, to fend to the *Englifh* Camp and enquire whether Mr. *de Chalons* was a Prifoner, and to defire he might be ranfom'd.

A GENTLEMAN of the Horfe, belonging to Mr. *de Granfon*, brought Mr. *de Vienne* the News of Madam *de Granfon*'s Arrival and of his Mafter's Death. Mr. *de Vienne*, who was prepar'd for it, and who befides, among the Variety of Duties, always reckon'd that of a Citizen one of the chief, went on in regulating, with Mr. *de Canaple*,

G 3   every

every Thing that was neceffary for the Defence of *Calais*. Being ftraitned for Time, Mr. *de Canaple* went away without fo much as endeavouring to make a Vifit to Madam *de Granfon*, whom it was not proper to fee in her prefent Circumftance. The Lofs of her Hufband had affected her more than it was natural for one to think it would; but the Heinoufnefs, as fhe thought, of never having lov'd him, and of having an Inclination towards another Man, help'd to blot out the ill Treatment fhe had receiv'd from him. She was moreover fenfible that to withftand her Weaknefs the Chains of Duty were of Service to her; this Liberty, which fhe could not make Ufe of, became a Weight difficult to bear.

MR. *de Vienne*, in Difcourfe, told her that Mr. *de Canaple*, in the fhort Stay he had made at *Calais*, had feen Mademoifelle *de Mailly*. The Perils of a Siege fill him with Apprehenfions, said

said he to her; he has advis'd me to cause all the Women of Distinction to depart the Place; and the better to Countenance his pressing me, with Regard to Mademoiselle *de Mailly*, he was very urgent with me on your Account: and indeed you would give me much Ease of Mind, pursu'd Mr. *de Vienne*, if you would retire to my Estate in *Burgundy*.

MADAM *de Granson* was in that Condition of Sorrow and Distress, wherein, by the Multiplicity of Misfortunes, we become fearless of any more. Do not deprive me of the only Satisfaction which is left me, said she to Mr. *de Vienne*, I can perish with you if it must be; though I am a Woman, you have nothing to fear from my Timorousness; but gratify Mr. *de Canaple*, and engage Mademoiselle *de Mailly* to go out of *Calais*. Mr. *de Vienne* promis'd he would endeavour so to do.

THE

THE Departure of Mademoiselle *de Mailly* would have been a Confolation to Madam *de Granfon*; fhe was not for having any Ting in common with Her, no not fo much as Misfortune itfelf; but Fate refus'd her even this poor Comfort. Madam *de Mailly*, whofe Paffions were violent, had conceiv'd fo much Difplea-fure at not being able to fatisfy Her Hatred and Revenge, fhe fell fick upon it. Mademoifelle *de Mailly* could not leave her Mother-in-law, and much lefs her Father, at fo unhappy a Conjun-cture. Mr. *de Vienne*, who had for Mr. *de Mailly* all the Regards which were due to his Birth, left him Mafter of his own Lot and to act juft as he pleas'd him-felf, as foon as he was made acquainted with his Reafons, and oblig'd no one of his Family to fubmit to the Order he had publifh'd; but all others that were ufelefs to the Defence of the Place were ordered to be gone.

EDWARD

EDWARD made no Delay to come before *Calais* and take a View of it; and being perfuaded he could not take it by Force, he refolv'd to ftarve it out. In this Defign, he form'd between the River *Haule* and the Sea, a Camp, which look'd like another Town. *Philip*, whofe Courage was not at all abated by the Lofs of the Battle of *Creffy*, prepar'd to ufe all Methods for faving fo important a Place. Mr. *de Canaple* had inform'd him, at his Return, that Mr. *de Vienne* would defend it to the laft Extremity, and give Time for getting together another Army. *Philip*, for the more expeditious raifing of Recruits, went from *Picardy*, and left for its Defence a Thoufand Men at Arms under the command of Mr. *de Canaple*.

THE Diligence which he had us'd to find out what had been the Fate of Mr. *de Chalons*, had prov'd ineffectual; but to avoid throwing Mademoifelle *de Mailly*

Maily into Defpair, he had poffefs'd her with Hopes which he had not himfelf.

TRUE it was however, that Mr. *de Chalons* was taken Prifoner. He had been found, after the Battle, under a Heap of Dead with fcarce any Remains of Life in him. My Lord *Arundel*, who was then on the Field of Battle, bufy'd in giving Relief to fuch as were yet in a Condition to receive it, judging by the Armour of Mr. *de Chalons* that he was a Perfon of Diftinction, order'd he fhould be carry'd into a private Tent. Some Papers which were found about him, and carry'd to my Lord *Arundel*, difcover'd to him the Name of the Prifoner, and much increas'd his Refpect for him. He imagin'd he might be of fome Service to him in a Matter which concern'd his Repofe. But as *Edward* would allow of no fending back of Prifoners, fo long as the War lafted, my Lord *Arundel* took Meafures for fecuring his to himfelf. He order'd a prudent

and

and faithful Retainer of his to keep him and attend him with all imaginable Care and Refpect.

HE was not for a long Time able to acknowlege, nor even to be fenfible of the good Treatment he receiv'd; his Wounds were fuch that more than once his Life was defpair'd of. When he was better, he defir'd to know into whofe Hands the Chance of War had thrown him; but thofe who were about him could not inform him. My Lord *Arundel*, for Fear he fhould difcover him, had only fent to know how he far'd; and deferr'd feeing him till he fhould be in a Condition to receive a Vifit from him. He had got him convey'd to a Peafant's Houfe, which he made as convenient as poffible, and where it was eafier to conceal him than in the Camp.

MY Lord *Arundel* went thither without any Attendants, as foon as his Pri-

foner

foner was able to receive him. It is with Pleafure I fee, faid he to him feat- ing himfelf by his Side, that the En- deavours we have ufed for preferving the Life of fo brave a Man have not been fruitlefs. What you have done to fave my Life, reply'd Mr. *de Chalons,* would not fully fatisfy your Generofity, if you did not likewife endeavour to lef- fen the Shame of my Defeat by the Elo- giums you beftow on a Bravery which has been of fo little Service to me; yet I don't know whether I can com- plain of a Misfortune which has put me in a way to be acquainted with fo gene- rous an Enemy.

Do not give me that Name, reply'd my Lord *Arundel*; our Kings wage War, Honour obliges us to follow them; but when we have no longer our Swords in our Hands, Humanity refumes its Rights, and the Valour which we have exercis'd againft one another in the Heat of the Fight becomes a frefh Mo- tive

tive of Esteem when it is at an End. That which I have for you did not wait for its Birth 'till I saw you in martial Array; your Merit has been long known to me, I have wish'd an Hundred Times to have a Friend like You, and Fortune could not do me a greater Service than the giving me a Kind of Claim to a Friendship, the Value whereof I was before-hand acquainted with.

If I am worthy to be your Friend, answer'd Mr. *de Chalons*, if you have any Esteem for me, you will believe me when I tell you that the Life you have so generously preserv'd is entirely at your Devotion: Yes, I am ready to sacrifice it to your Service; and that not so much to discharge the Debt I owe you, as to gratify the Love and Admiration which your noble Procedure inspires me with. Leave me no longer ignorant of my Benefactor's Name: Pray inform me how I came to be known to you, and by what

what good Fortune you have conceiv'd of me so favourable an Idea.

MY Name is *Arundel*, reply'd he; as to what you farther desire to know of me, I cannot satisfy you without giving you an Account of Part of my Life. You will see by the Assistance which I shall beg of you, and by the Importance of the Things which I have to tell you, that my Confidence stands in no Need of being supported by a more particular Knowledge. But the Recital of this, pursu'd he rising up to take his Leave, requires more Time than I have at present; besides, I am afraid of fatiguing you by too long an Attention.

MR. *Arundel* had Reason to think his Prisoner was in no Condition to hear him. No sooner was the Name of *Arundel* pronounc'd but he was seiz'd with a Trembling all over him to that Degree, that the People, to whose Care he

was

was committed, could not but take Notice of it, and haften'd to his Relief;
but their Tenderneſs, which he only
ow'd to an odious Hand, was rejected
with a Kind of Rage ; he order'd them,.
with ſo reſolute a Tone, to leave him
to himſelf, that they were forc'd to o-
bey.

INTO what an Abyſs of Diſaſters
did he ſee himſelf plung'd! This Man
who had deſtroy'd his whole Felicity,
this Man, to whom he had ſo juſt an
Hatred, was the ſame who had ſav'd his
Life, and who had quite overcome him
with the Generoſity and Frankneſs of
his Behaviour. He aſks my Aſſiſtance, ſaid he, in all Appearance to tear
my very Heart from me, and cut the
Strings of Life! For what other Occaſion can he have for me but that of ſerv-
ing him in his Love?

So then! I am ſo perfectly forgot
that he has never heard my Name pronounc'd

nounc'd, he has not had me to contend with in the Heart he has robb'd me of, but enjoys the Pleaſure of believing he alone has been belov'd! But I will take that Pleaſure from him; he ſhall know that I have been his Rival, and he ſhall know it at the Expence of his Life.

THESE Views of Revenge, ſo little becoming the Honour of Mr. *de Chalons*, could not laſt long. He was firſt to acquit himſelf of his Obligations to my Lord *Arundel* before he acted as an Enemy. The War might perhaps afford him a Means of doing this; but he was not free, and he would not owe his Freedom to an Enemy: He might offer him a moſt extravagant Ranſom; would it be accepted? And if it was not, what Courſe ſhould he take? Again, would Honour allow him to give Ear to the Secrets intended to be committed to him? It is true he might thereby come at ſome Lights which imported his Repoſe.

I

I SHALL know, said he, what it fo much concerns me to know; I fhall know why I am betray'd. Alas! recalling himfelf, what need have I to hunt after any other Caufes of it, than the natural Inconftancy of Women! My Lord *Arundel* has Matter, more than enough, to juftify it. He was prefent, I was abfent; he has been belov'd, I have been forgot.

THE whole Heart of Mr. *de Chalons* was fhock'd at this Idea, and he accus'd himfelf with doing a mortal Wrong to Mademoifelle *de Mailly*. Can I know her by this Weaknefs? faid he. Ought I to fufpect Her, of all Women, to be capable of being led away by outward Advantages, by a Perfon's Figure? Do I not know that the Happinefs I had to pleafe her, was owing to fome Virtue which fhe thought fhe difcern'd in me?

THE

THE Anxiety, the Agitation of Mind, and the different Sentiments with which Mr. *de Chalons* was fill'd, did not permit him to be long before he determin'd what to do. That whole Night and Part of the following Day were spent in deploring the Unhappiness of his Condition. He at last concluded to hear what it was Mr. *Arundel* had to say to him, and regulate thereupon his Measures; firmly resolving, whatever he might hear, carefully to conceal his having been belov'd. The Affection which she has for me, said he, is a Secret which she entrusted to me, and which no Reason will authorize me to violate; and it was not without Shame he recollected his having thought differently in the first Moments of his Surprise and Sorrow.

THE Trouble he was in, receiv'd an Addition. Word was brought him that a Woman, conducted by my Lord *Arundel*'s People, desir'd to speak with
him;

him; she was no sooner brought into the Chamber but she fell on her Knees by Mr. *de Chalons*'s Bed-side, and presented to him, in the most moving Manner, a young Child she held in her Arms. I have lost every Thing, said she to him pouring forth Abundance of Tears, I am driven from my native Country, I have left *Calais*, my Brothers, my Husband, my Father, expos'd to all the Horrors of War and of Famine; I have no Hope but in your Assistance, I am come to ask it of you in the Name of this Infant, whom I have preserv'd to you amidst so many Perils.

THE violent Passions which had in some Degree been quell'd by the Reflexions he had just been making, were at this Sight reviv'd with a fresh Force in the Soul of Mr. *de Chalons*. Be gone, said he with a Tone which discovered both Anger and Grief; take from my Eyes this wretched Creature, the Fruit of the most abominable Treachery. The

The Woman, affrighted at what she heard, remain'd motionless, and the unhappy Child spread forth its little Arms to embrace Mr. *de Chalons*, and call'd him by the Name of Father.

THIS Name gave Increase to the Sorrow which before had pierc'd him to the Soul. The Happiness of him to whom so indearing a Name did of Right belong, imprinted itself more lively in his Imagination, and not being able to support such racking Ideas, he thrust aside this innocent Creature, and directing himself to the Woman who was still on her Knees, Once more, said he to her, get away and never let me see you again; and making a Sign to those who waited on him to put her out, he turn'd himself to the other Side, with a Heart full of Grief, Anger, and Revenge.

THIS Event was not likely to make any Change in his Situation; he had
been

been long before no Stranger to that
which was the Subject of his Deſpair,
but Time had weaken'd thoſe Ideas.
The Knowledge of my Lord *Arundel*
had already but too ſadly re-trac'd them
in his Memory; they were now a-
waken'd again in a yet more violent
Manner.

AFTER many Uncertainties and
Strugglings, his natural Temper, which
in the Main was of a ſoft Caſt, at
Length prevail'd. The extreme Love
which he had for Mademoiſelle *de
Mailly* inſpir'd him likewiſe with ſome
Compaſſion for her Child; a Senſe of
Juſtice join'd itſelf to his Compaſſion.
Why ſhould he gratify his Vengeance
at the Expence of this unfortunate
little one? Is he guilty of his Birth, he
does not ſo much as know it? What
Right had he to raviſh it from its Pa-
rents? Were it not better to reſtore it to
him he judg'd to be its Father? He
thereby diſcharg'd the Debt of Gratitude

tude which he ow'd him, that Gratitude which was not the leaft grievous of all his Afflictions. It was neceffary, before all Things, to hear the Story which my Lord *Arundel* was to relate to him. But how could he fupport this terrible Confidence? Would he be Mafter of himfelf and of his Paffion? Could he be able to hear Things, the very Idea whereof made him tremble? What matters it after all? faid he, I can but die, and Death is preferable to the Diftraction I am in.

MR. *de Chalons*, in Purfuance of thefe Refolutions, gave the neceffary Orders, and difpos'd himfelf to receive my Lord *Arundel*.

End of the Second Part, and of the Firft Volume.

THE
SIEGE of *CALAIS*,

BY

EDWARD of ENGLAND.

VOL. II.

PART III.

MY Lord *Arundel*, detained by the Bufinefs of the War, could not, till after fome Days, gratify the Defire he had to fee his Prifoner again. Can you attend now to what I have to tell you? faid he to him entering his Chamber, and feating himfelf by him.

him. Mr. *de Chaions* anfwered fome Words with a trembling Voice, which my Lord *Arundel* attributed to the weak Condition he might ftill be in; and being unwilling to lofe Moments fo precious to him, he thus befpoke him.

I HAD fcarce finifhed my Exercifes, when EDWARD, for political Reafons, refolved to marry me to Mademoifelle *Hamilton*; he hoped, by forming Alliances between the chief Families of *England* and *Scotland*, to unite by degrees the two Nations. My Father fell in with the King's Views. As they did not mean to ufe Authority for obtaining the Confent of the *Hamilton* Family, and that Mademoifelle *Hamilton*'s tender Age afforded Time enough to obtain it; the King's Defign remained a Secret between my Father and Him.

I WAS fent to *Guyenne*; the Peace which was then between the Two Crowns, made me defirous to fee the
Court

Court of *France.* I there contracted a
Friendship with the young *Soyecourt,*
whose Character suited my Temper
more than that of any other young
Men of my Age with whom I had kept
Company. I met with him again at
Calais, where I had proposed to make
some Stay. He was fond of doing me
the Honours of the Town. Madam *de
Mailly's* being the most considerable
House, I was received there, and enter-
tained as One whose Name entitled him
to some Distinction.

SOYECOURT proposed to me a
few Days after to go to an Abbey, a
quarter of a League from the Town,
where a young Lady was to take the
Veil. I consented to it; we found the
Church full of People of Condition :
The Crowd was great, and the Heat
excessive. I got as near as I could to
the Place where the Ceremony was performing. A young Lady who had
some Employ therein, but whose Face I

H　　　　　could

could not fee by reafon of a Veil which partly covered it, fell into a Swoon.

EVERY body was forward to help her, and I among the reft: I made her take fome of a fpirituous Liquor which I chanced to have about me: but that did no Service towards bringing her to herfelf again; it was neceffary to give her Air; I helped to carry her out of the Church; her Head-drefs, which this Accident had difordered, let fall on her Face and Neck the fineft fair Hair in the World, in natural Curls; her Eyes, though clofed, gave Paffage to fome Tears. The fhort precipitate Sighs which fhe fent forth every Moment, the Sweetnefs of her Vifage, her Age, which feemed hardly to have reached fixteen Years, All this rendered her to the utmoft Degree affecting.

MADEMOISELLE *de Mailly*, whom I had before feen at her Mother-in-law's, came to her Affiftance, and did it with
fuch

ſuch Teſtimonies of Friendſhip, as engaged my Thanks full as much as any
Service ſhe could have done myſelf. It
ſeemed to me as if the Condition of this
young Lady created in the former a ſort
of Compaſſion, different from what one
feels for ſo tranſient an Illneſs; I thought
too that I heard her ſpeak ſome Words of
Conſolation to her.

SOYECOURT, who was not at
firſt aware of this Accident, came running to us like one diſtracted. At this
Inſtant ſhe began to recover her Senſes:
She faintly caſt her Eyes on all around
her, and I being a Stranger to her, ſhe
fixed them on Me. Her Countenance,
the moſt beautiful in the World and
the moſt touching, became more ſo by
the Sadneſs which ſpread itſelf all over
it; I was ſtruck with deep Concern,
and, even then, What would I not have
done to alleviate her Sufferings? Mademoiſelle *de Mailly*, after whiſpering
ſome Words to her, and thanking us

for our kind Affiftance, took her under her Arm, and went with her into the Houfe ; whither we were not permitted to follow her.

SOYECOURT and myfelf ftayed together fome time ; the Condition I had feen him in when he had joined us, gave me a Sufpicion he was in Love, and a certain Impreffion which I began to be fenfible of in myfelf, fpurred me to find out the Truth.

WHO is this Perfon, for whom you juft now difcovered fo much Concern ? faid I to him. It is, replied he, Mademoifelle *de Roye*, a Niece of Madam *de Mailly*'s ; She has no Fortune, mine depends on an Uncle who will never let me marry a Woman without one. Notwithftanding all thefe Obftacles, I am fallen in Love, and am the more to be pitied, as inftead of being able to contribute to her Happinefs, I am on the contrary afraid the Refpect I have fhewn

for

for her, has haftened her being forced into a Cloifter.

I T was not enough for me to know that *Soyecourt* was in Love, it was like-wife neceffary to know whether he was beloved. I cannot flatter myfelf that I am, faid he to me, I believe I might have loved her ten Years without her vouchfafing to take any Notice of it; and when I have mentioned it, fhe never troubled herfelf to conteft the Sincerity of my Paffion.

I A M willing to believe you, faid fhe to me, provided You will believe Me in like manner. My Condition and my Fortune would fuffice to throw an invincible Obftacle in the Way of your Pretenfions; but this Obftacle, though invincible, is not however fo ftrong, but there is another yet ftronger. I know not whether I was born infenfible, and formed, as it were, of Marble, but Your Endeavours and your Love have

H 3   made

made no Impreſſion on my Heart. I
did not, adds *Soyecourt*, abide by this
firſt Declaration, I have uſed all Methods, and All have proved ineffectual;
ſhe hears me with a Mildneſs a thouſand
times more grievous than her Severities
would be.

Do you not ſee, would ſhe ſay to me
ſometimes, that you have made all the
Progreſs you can make with me? I
think you amiable, I eſteem you, I believe you have a real Value for me, and
yet all this does not touch me, does not
reach to my Heart: Get rid of a Fancy
which makes you unhappy, and give
me no longer the Affliction, for ſuch it
is to me, to ſee you ſo diſordered.

My Curioſity increaſed in proportion
as *Soyecourt* went on in his Diſcourſe;
the minuteſt Particulars ſeemed to me of
Moment. But, ſaid I, perhaps it is Mademoiſelle *de Roye*'s Prudence which is
the greateſt Obſtacle, and if ſhe ſaw
                                    any

any Poffibility of your ever marrying her, fhe would treat you in another Manner. Do not think, replied he, that I have neglected this Method ; though my Eftate is none of the largeft, yet it may be called an Eafy Fortune. I am moreover convinced, that my Uncle's Refentment would not hold out againft the Charms and Character of Mademoifelle *de Roye*, and I have told her as much with all the Strength of Perfuafion and all the Energy of a lively Paffion.

You rely too much on the Power of my Charms, would fhe anfwer me, and though I fhould rely thereon as much as you do, I fhould be never the more difpofed to accept of your Propofals. My whole Heart would hardly fuffice to difcharge the Debt I fhould owe you. Sentiments of Efteem and Gratitude would be but a poor Return for yours ; and I fhould be always upbraiding myfelf with being Ungrateful,

H 4 nor

nor could I ever be able to ceaſe to be ſo.

EVERY thing which *Soyecourt* ſaid, painted to me Mademoiſelle *de Roye* ſo amiable for a noble Freedom, which perhaps was peculiar to herſelf alone, that he completed by his Diſcourſe the Impreſſion which her Perſon had already made on me. An Inſenſible Fairone piqued my Self-love, and though I did not indeed conceive myſelf to have more intrinſick Worth than *Soyecourt,* I perſuaded myſelf that I could love better, and that the Vivacity and Warmth of my Paſſion would furniſh me with ſuch Means of Pleaſing as He could not employ. The Friendſhip which was between us, raiſed no Scruple in me : I could do him no Wrong, ſince he was not Beloved.

I WENT, as ſoon as I could, to Madam *de Mailly*'s ; Mademoiſelle *de Mailly* was with her : I aſked after Made-

Mademoiselle *de Roye*'s Health. How! said Madam *de Mailly* turning to her, does the Gentleman know of the Accident which befell *Amelia*? He was a Witness of it, answered Mademoiselle *de Mailly*, and it was partly owing to his Endeavours that Mademoiselle *de Roye* was brought to herself again. Methinks, said Madam *de Mailly*, in a Tone not unmixed with some Sharpness, it had been properer for *Amelia* to be assisted by Persons of the Convent, than by a Man of Mr. *Arundel*'s Age and Figure. She is not far off, said she to me; Mademoiselle *de Mailly*, who has a Kindness for her, has desired me to send to fetch her.

MADEMOISELLE *de Roye* shewed herself some Moments the next Day in her Aunt's Chamber; though she looked much dispirited and very melancholy, she seemed to me never the less lovely for that, nay, perhaps the more so. Madam *de Mailly* had her Eye pretty

H 5   much

much upon me. I perceived it, and did that Violence to myself as not to look on Mademoiselle *de Roye*, and to say nothing to her farther than Good Manners required. For her part, she durst hardly lift up her Eyes and pronounce a few Words.

MEAN while I was imperceptibly grown into Favour with Madam *de Mailly*, and I endeavoured to be more so, with a View to employ it for Mademoiselle *de Roye*. I had seen as much as convinced me, that her Aunt used her barbarously. I succeeded in my Design far beyond my Expectation. Madam *de Mailly* shewed me upon all Occasions certain soothing Distinctions, yet still preserving that austere Air which doubtless she had contracted a Habit of.

SOYECOURT durst never appear at the House but at such Times as all Comers were admitted, and then Mademoiselle *de Roye* was hardly ever there.

He

He often talked to me of his Sufferings; I might have paid him Confidence for Confidence, and have taken the Counſel I gave him, to labour to cure himſelf; but his Misfortune, inſtead of diſheartening me, ſeemed to encourage me; and then, to tell you the Truth, I was forced away by an Inclination ſtronger than any Reflexions. Without having any determined Deſign, without conſidering what would be the Conſequences of my Paſſion, I delivered myſelf wholly up to it.

MR. *de Mouy,* *Soyecourt*'s Uncle, alarmed at his Nephew's Love, came to *Calais* to fetch him away. Madam *de Mailly,* whom he was acquainted with, diſplayed to his Eyes a Reaſonableneſs and a Generoſity, which the Hatred ſhe bore to her Niece made it very eaſy for her to exert.

I HAVE oppoſed, ſaid ſhe to him, as much as I poſſibly could, Mr. *de*

Soyecourt's Inclination; it is to prevent its Consequences that I have pressed Mademoiselle *de Roye* to execute a Resolution she is in, of going into a Convent, the only Course that can suit such a young Creature as she. If you would be ruled by me, added Madam *de Mailly*, you will get Mr. *de Soyecourt* away; he must by no means be Witness of a Ceremony which may soften him yet more.

A PROCEDURE which had such specious and plausible Motives, gained her the Admiration and Thanks of Mr. *de Mouy*. In order to correspond therewith, he thought it His Part to speak to Mademoiselle *de Roye* himself, and to lay before her his Reasons for opposing his Nephew's Design.

MADEMOISELLE *de Roye* received his Reasons with so much Temper, so much Judgment, so much Truth, that He, who always had the greatest Aversion fion to the very Thoughts of Marrying, became fenfible that a Perfon of this Character would make a Hufband perfectly happy. The Beauty of Mademoifelle *de Roye* finifhed what her Good Senfe had begun; and the Uncle, fome Days after, was as deeply in Love as the Nephew. Although this Step ran counter to all his paft Conduct, he refolved to propofe Himfelf to her.

So advantageous an Offer, fet in parallel with a Cloifter, whereto Mademoifelle *de Roye* feemed to have no natural Inclination, left no Room for Mr. *de Mouy* to doubt but that his Propofal would be received with Joy. How great was his Aftonifhment to find Mademoifelle *de Roye* in quite different Sentiments! Think not, faid fhe, that a fecret Inclination to Mr. *de Soyecourt* is the Caufe of my Refufal; to convince you of this, I will immediately go and renounce the World.

I WAS

I WAS so often at Madam *de Mailly's*, that it was hardly possible not to know what was transacting. Mademoiselle *de Mailly*, who honoured me with a Share of her Friendship and of her Confidence, had told me in part how Matters stood, and Madam *de Mailly* informed me of every thing which I was ignorant of. One Day as I was alone with the latter, and was saying such fine Things to her as the Fashion allows of; You treat me too much like other Women, said she to me: What is it you mean by these Gallantries? You know I ought not so much as to hear them; my whole Affection is due to Mr. *de Mailly*. I must however own, that though my Confidence is very great towards him, there are a Thousand Things which, for the Sake of his Repose, I am obliged to conceal from him. I should be glad to have a Friend so Trusty, that I may say to him what I do not to Mr. *de Mailly*, and so Prudent as to advise

me

me in the Management of nice Affairs.

THE Qualifications which were wanted in this Friend, were the same which I had often been commended for myself; I saw by this Preamble and all that had preceded, that it was wished I would be this Friend. It was necessary to say what was expected from me; my Heart, at bottom, startled at it; but there are Cases wherein the honestest Man finds himself forced to act beyond what he would willingly do. And now behold me linked with Madam *de Mailly*; as I had several times declared that I should stay in *France* as long as my Father should stay in *Scotland*, where his Abode was to be for a considerable Time, the Fear of my Absence brought no Obstacle to our Correspondence.

SOME time after this Conversation, she desired me to come to her at an Hour when I should meet with no other
Person

Person whatever. I am, said she to me, in one of those Circumstances I told you of; I have a Thousand Griefs which I should smother in my Bosom, if I had not the Liberty of imparting them to You. The Interest of my Son engaged me in a second Marriage: Mademoiselle *de Mailly* was to be the Price of my Compliance ; she asked Time to resolve, that Time is expired; yet she comes to no Determination ; nay, she seems to affect treating Mr. *de Boulai* worse than she did at first. Mr. *de Mailly* has not the Power to make himself be Obeyed; I have at one and the same time the Grief of my Son to support, and also the Shame of having made a fruitless Step : I find too in other Respects nothing but Opposition to whatever I go about. Mademoiselle *de Roye* takes it in her Head to refuse the Offers of Mr. *de Mouy*, who, unhappily for him, is in Love with her, and who is so bewitched as to desire to marry her. The Heroism which she pranks

herself

herfelf up with, does not deceive me ;
fhe furely loves *Soyecourt*, and keeps
herfelf for him. Mademoifelle *de Mailly*
and She are in each Others Secrets ; for
Women are never knit together but by
fuch fort of Confidence. Thefe Perfons
who feem fo difcreet and rational, are
nothing lefs than what they feem to
be.

THE Envy and Jealoufy of Madam
de Mailly exercifed themfelves in the
Picture which fhe drew of the one and
the other, and confirmed me in the bad
Opinion I had before conceived of her
Character, which I found in all Refpects
to be very different from that which
fhe affumed to herfelf in the Eye of the
World.

As I was far from making Advantage of her Weakneffes, her Expref-
fions were taken literally ; I did not go
out of the Bounds of Friendfhip, and I
thought thereby to preferve to myfelf a
Right

Right of declaring to her, when I had a Mind, my Paſſion for Mademoiſelle *de Roye*.

THE Suſpicions which had been juſt infuſed into me, of her loving *Soyecourt*, made a deep Impreſſion upon me ; I was much troubled and alarmed thereat ; the Things he had ſaid to me, and which in a manner made me eaſy, ceaſed to do ſo now : I imagined they concealed from him his good Fortune. Mademoiſelle *de Roye* had touched me chiefly becauſe I had thought her invulnerable to the Darts of Love ; the Diſcovery of a Rival beloved, quite changed all my Notions, yet did not change my Heart. I had till then beheld her without daring to attempt to ſpeak to her ; I now was of Opinion I owed her leſs Regard and leſs Reſpect ; and had not her Departure for the Convent deprived me of the Means, I believe I ſhould have proceeded ſo far in my Folly as to rail againſt her to her Face.

MADAM

MADAM *de Mailly*, overjoyed at getting her removed, conducted her herself into the Place of her Retirement. I came a Moment after they were set out. Mademoiselle *de Mailly* was in Tears; her Grief extorted Lamentations from her, 'which till then she had smothered on Madam *de Mailly*'s Account. You are in Favour with her, said she, why do you not inspire her with gentler Sentiments? What Barbarity is it, to oblige this unhappy Maid to bury herself alive!

THE Tears of Mademoiselle *de Mailly* then flowed in abundance. I seemed to her to be so much concerned thereat, nay, I was really so to that Degree, that I had no Difficulty to persuade her she might depend upon me. We deliberated together what was fit to be done; we concluded she should go the next Day to see her Friend, that she should concert with her the Course which should

should be taken, and that she should give me an Account thereof.

ALTHOUGH my Suspicions as to *Soyecourt* subsisted, I was not the less disposed to serve Mademoiselle *de Roye* ; she was too much to be pitied to refuse her my Aid, and I should have given it her, even though she had really offended me. Madam *de Mailly* found me when she returned, at her House ; she put on a Sadness which covered a malicious Joy ; I perceived it, for all her Art and Dissimulation, and it filled me with Resentment, which however I kept from breaking out. It was more than ever necessary Not to displease her.

SHE did not dare to constrain her Daughter-in-law to a certain Degree, and therefore it was easy for me to speak with her. I know not how it is, said she to me at her Return from the Visit we had agreed upon, Mademoiselle *de Roye*

Roye is abfolutely changed; the feeing of a Ceremony which interefted her no otherwife than as it might give her a too lively Idea perhaps of the like which would one Day be done on her Account, threw her into the Condition wherein you faw her and fuccoured her; and Now fhe feems to be impatient for the Arrival of a Moment fhe then fo much dreaded. I am affrighted at her Tranquillity; fhe fets before my Eyes a Soul above its Misfortune, only becaufe it forefees the End of it. What a Profpect for fo accomplifhed a Maiden, to have in View no other Change of her Fortune but Death!

WHAT Mademoifelle *de Mailly* faid to me, made me fhudder, and fhe was affected in the fame Manner herfelf. Alas! faid fhe, if the Perfecutions which are inflicted on me to make me marry Mr. *du Boulai* continue, I fhall foon take the fame Courfe, and I fhall not take it with lefs Repugnance; for I am

fure

fure Mademoifelle *de Roye* is ftill in the
fame Way of Thinking fhe always was.
Thofe Trifles, thofe little Nothings
which fill the Heads of your cloiftered
Women, can find no Place in hers;
fhe will be unhappy, for want of being
able to make continual Sacrifices of
Reafon and Good-Senfe. Let us there-
fore prevent her, faid I, from putting
herfelf under a Neceffity of making
thofe Sacrifices; do you perfuade her
to wait the Succefs of our Endeavours,
and prevail on her to do nothing
rafhly.

IN this Situation Things remained
fome Days. Mean while Madam *de
Mailly* could in no wife brook my dif-
courfing fo often and fo long with Mademoifelle *de Mailly*. You are going,
faid fhe to me, to fuffer yourfelf to be
led away by Mademoifelle *de Mailly's*
wanton Airs; confider that fhe is engaged to my Son, and that you would
difappoint me more Ways than One.

IT

4

IT had been no difficult Matter for me to remove her Fears; I was not in Love with Mademoiselle *de Mailly*, and the Truth always makes itself be felt; but, in order to justify myself perfectly, I must have made Declarations no less opposite to my Thoughts than to my Character. Besides, the Restraints I laid myself under with this Woman, became more and more irksome to me, in proportion to my gaining a better Knowledge of her; and had it not been for Reasons which kept me to her, I should have ceased visiting her.

SOYECOURT was left at *Paris*; he came every Day to relate his Disconsolations to me. One Morning He entered my Chamber, with Grief and Despair imprinted on his Face. You have seen me, said he, very miserable: you have seen a Maid I adore, ready to be snatched from me by an Uncle, and with her my whole Fortune; this
same

fame Maid prefers a Cloifter, where I lofe her for ever, before a Settlement which I fancied fhe refufed purely out of a Sentiment of Generofity, which rendered the Lofs of her ftill more fenfible and grievous. Are not thefe Afflictions heavy enough? and would you think it was in the Power of Fortune to invent others to fink an Unhappy Wretch to a lower Degree of Mifery? She has found out the Secret for me. My Uncle, moved at my Defpair, moved with Pity for Mademoifelle *de Roye,* has made his Love give way to Sentiments more worthy of him; he is gone, without acquainting me, to tell her, that he not only confented to our Marriage, but that he begged it of her, as a Favour, that fhe would confent to it herfelf. The Refufal which I have made, faid fhe to him, of what you were pleafed to offer me, has impofed on me a Law, not to accept of any farther Offer. Befides, my Choice is made, my Refolution

lution is taken, and can never more be changed.

My Uncle, continued *Soyecourt*, at the same time as he related to me what I have told you, doubted not but my Speaking to her would be of more Force than his, and that I ſhould determine Mademoiſelle *de Roye* in my Favour. I ran to her Convent: She had not ſeen me but for the repeated Inſtances of the Superior of the Houſe, whom I had diſcourſed, and whom my extreme Affliction had brought over to my Intereſts. Will you then forſake me, ſaid I to her, throwing myſelf at her Feet? Am I ſo hateful to you, that you ſhould rather chooſe the Horror of this Solitude? Why do you deſire my Death? Why do you deſire your own? For you will never ſupport the Way of Life you are going to embrace. In Pity to yourſelf, aſſume more humane Sentiments. Can it be ſo terrible a Thing to you, to unite yourſelf with a Man
I   whom

whom you honour with some Degree of Esteem, and by whom you well know you are adored?

YES, I do know it, said she, lifting upon me Eyes not unbedewed with Tears; and it is the Certainty I have of it which obliges me to refuse you. Could you be content without the Possession of my Heart? Would you not have a Right to reproach me with Ingratitude? And, even though You should never reproach me, should I reproach myself the less for that? and could I ever forgive it myself?

WHAT have I not said to her! pursued *Soyecourt*. Alas! I have said but too much to her; it is the Pity which I inspired her with, that has forced her to own to me what I would gladly, at the Expence of my Life, have always been ignorant of. She is in love; she has a secret Inclination which constitutes her Misfortune, as well as Mine. It is to hide her

her Weakneſs, it is to puniſh herſelf for it, that ſhe embraces, almoſt with Joy, the monaſtic State.

SOYECOURT's Words gave me at once much Curioſity and much Emotion. I wanted to know who this fortunate Rival was; but *Soyecourt* was not inform'd of that, nor did he know himſelf on whom to place his Suſpicions. Mademoiſelle *de Roye* had ſaid that her fatal Secret was known to nobody, and that he who was the Object of it ſhould never have any Knowlege thereof. In depriving me of Hope, continu'd *Soyecourt*, ſhe the more increaſes my Admiration for her.

I will be gone far from a Place which would no longer offer me any Thing but Subjects of Sorrow; and I will expect from Time and Reflexions a Repoſe which perhaps I ſhall never recover.

I 2 THE

THE Design which he form'd, left me in full Liberty to follow my Inclination. As soon as I was alone, I fell to revolving in my Mind all that I had juft heard; I confider'd the Procedure of of Mademoifelle *de Roye*; I weigh'd efpecially every Thing which I had feen; I brought together a Thoufand little Nothings, to which I durft not give a favourable Interpretation, and which then begot in me fome Hopes and gave me a Senfation of Joy and Pleafure, which the Fear of deceiving myfelf put a Stop to. I was abfolutely bent on fatisfying my Doubts, being fully refolv'd, if I was belov'd, to efpoufe Mademoifelle *de Roye*, and to run the Hazard, if it was neceffary, of expofing myfelf to the King's utmoft Refentment for breaking my Engagement with Mademoifelle *Hamilton.*

To come at this Difcovery, I at firft could devife no Method but what feemed

ed

ed full of Infuperable Difficulties. At
length, after having well examin'd what
might be fufceptible of fome Poffibility,
I found the beft Way would be to intro-
duce myfelf into the Convent. The
Difficulties of the Enterprife did not
ftop me ; I was fure to level them. I
won over to my Intereft the Gardiner
and all the Women that had the keeping of the Gate; but I was not much
the forwarder for that: An Opportunity
was neceffary, and Chance befriended me.

I HAD heard at Madam *de Mailly's*
that they were to carry fome Furniture to
Mademoifelle *de Roye.* I prefently repair'd to the Friends I had made; we
agreed they fhould take in the Furniture,
and, that, as they could not put it up
without Help, I fhould be employ'd
therein. We pitch'd upon the Time
when the Nuns were detain'd in the
Choir. And now behold us on our
March; the Gardiner, the Gatekeepers,

and

and myfelf, each laden with their refpe-
ctive Burthen. When they had laid down
theirs, they left me in the Chamber,
where I was very bufy in exercifing a
Trade I little underftood.

MADEMOISELLE *de Roye* came in
foon after, without almoft perceiving
me, without concerning herfelf at all
with what I was doing. She threw herfelf on a Chair, leaning her Head on
one of her Hands, with which fhe cover'd her Eyes, and gave herfelf up to
a moft profound Penfivenefs. My
Diforder was extremely great; I had no
longer the Power to improve fo precious
a Moment. The Step I had taken appear'd to me the Height of Extrava-
gance; I was violating the Azylum of
a Convent, I was come to furprize a
young Lady alone in her Chamber, to
fpeak to her of a Paffion of which I
had never given her the leaft Knowlege;
and upon what Foundation was I to fpeak
to her of it? Upon a frivolous Hope
that

that she was touch'd with an Inclination for me.

THESE Reflexions would have restrain'd me, and I had gone away without discovering myself; but Mademoiselle *de Roye* was so beautiful; I saw her so Melancholy; this Melancholy pictur'd to me in such lively Colours the State of her Soul, and the fatal Consequences which Mademoiselle *de Mailly* had exhibited to my View, that yielding myself up entirely to the Sway of my Love, I went and threw myself at her Feet. Her Trouble and Affright were so extreme, that I might have had Time to say to her in this first Moment every Thing that could justify, or at least excuse, my Proceeding; but the Fear I saw she was in represented to me, nay exaggerated to me in so strong a Manner the Danger to which I expos'd her, and I was myself in so much Disorder, that I could hardly bring out a few Words, badly articulated and worse connected.

O MY

O MY GOD! what have I done to you? cry'd she at last with a trembling Voice and with a Visage wherein Affright was pictur'd. Was I not sufficiently wretched! Leave me, answer'd she, or you will make me die. These Words and the Air with which she deliver'd them, which seem'd to ask me Pardon, pierc'd me to the Heart, and left me not the Liberty of disobeying her; when one of the Women, who had introduc'd me, came in a great Hurry, to tell us Madam *de Mailly* was coming. She was so near entering that it was necessary to think of hiding me somewhere in the Chamber. The most proper, and the only Place, was a Kind of Port-hole of a Window, with a Curtain drawn before it. Here I pass'd the most painful Hour I ever pass'd in my Life. Madam *de Mailly* made no Motion that did not startle me. Mademoiselle *de Roye*, pale, speechless, and in a Condition very little different from

one

one at the Point of Death, affected me
with a Compassion which still aug-
mented the tender Interest I took in her;
I would have redeem'd with my Blood the
Anxiety I occasion'd to her. But what
was my Indignation, when I heard the
harsh Manner in which Madam *de Mailly*
spoke to her, the Cruelty with which
she press'd her to take the Veil, and all
the sharp, and even shocking Things she
added to determine her thereto!

How dangerous soever it would have
been to me to be discover'd in a Place
so severely forbidden to Men, I was
ready twenty Times to shew myself, to
declare that I offer'd Mademoiselle *de
Roye* my Hand, if she pleas'd to accept
of it. Nothing withheld me but the
Fear of obstructing my Design by discovering it. I was also afraid of making
a Noise in the World, which would have
been displeasing to Mademoiselle *de Roye*,
whatever the Event had been.

SHE

SHE was a confiderable Time without fpeaking. At length, committing, as it feem'd to me, a Violence on her Grief: I will obey you, Madam, fays fhe to her. Madam *de Mailly*, fatisfy'd with this Promife, went out. Mademoifelle *de Roye* waited on her, and fent my Confidante to let me know fhe would not return into her Chamber fo long as I was there.

I PATIENTLY fubmitted, and went Home to write to her, not a Letter but a Volume. The Danger to which I had expos'd her, made me more enamour'd, and render'd her a Thoufand Times more dear to me. That Voice, full of Charms, was ftill in my Ear, faying to me, with a Tone wherein Fear alone bore Sway, *O my God! what have I done to you!* I cannot reprefent to you how greatly I was imprefs'd thereby, and how much my Softnefs gain'd upon me.

I HAD

I HAD no Anſwer to that Letter, nor
to ſeveral others which I wrote afterwards. At laſt I ſent her Word, that
if ſhe would not be ſo good as to hear
what I had to offer, ſhe would put me
upon ſuch another Attempt as the former. Perhaps ſhe magnify'd to herſelf
the Danger I might expoſe her to. Be-
ſides, Decency ſuffer'd no Damage, as I
only deſir'd to ſee her at the Grate, and
at laſt ſhe conſented to it.

I NEVER paſs'd a Time more agreeable, and yet more hard to paſs, than that
which preceded the Day fix'd for this
Interview. The Pleaſure of ſeeing Mademoiſelle *de Roye*, of ſeeing her with
her own Conſent, the Hope of determining
her in my Favour, the Schemes I laid
for the future, fill'd my Heart with a
Joy which ſpred itſelf over all my A-
ctions; but my Impatience was ſo extremely great, it gave me ſo much Inquietude, that it was not poſſible for me

I 6   to

to fit ftill a Moment. I could continue
no where; I fancy'd by fhifting from
Place to Place I fhould fhorten the
Day.

THAT which I expected, at laft arriv'd. Though I was in a vaft Agitation, and my Heart beat violently,
when I found myfelf over-againft Mademoifelle *de Roye*, I had not the
fame Perplexity, nor the fame Fear as at
the firft Time. The little I had faid to
her Then, the Letters I had written to
her Afterwards, had embolden'd me.

MADEMOISELLE *de Roye* on the contrary feem'd to be more fearful and more
perplex'd. What did not I fay to her?
How many Proteftations, Oaths, nay
Tears, and Tears too fincere not to
make an Impreffion! What fhall I fay
to you? It was my Heart which fpoke;
it perfuaded a Heart, which my good
Fortune had prepoffefs'd favourably for
me. After much Refiftance, I obtain'd
Leave

Leave to come again in some Days. I could not prevail on myself to wait the Time assign'd me; I return'd the very next Day. Faults of this Kind are easily pardon'd; I was chid, indeed, for not Obeying, but chid in so mild a Manner that it was next Kin to thanking me.

IN Spite of Madam *de Mailly*'s Orders, our Interviews became easy. And now having no more Occasion to use Stratagems with Mademoiselle *de Roye*, I took my Measures so well, and had so well secur'd to my Interest those who were necessary to me, that there hardly pass'd a Day but I spent at least some Moments at this happy Grate.

THE Character of Mademoiselle *de Roye* leaves nothing wanting to secure the Felicity of a Lover, and the Tranquility of a Husband. Her Discourse, her whole Conduct breathes Truth; she is a Stranger to the Desire of Pleasing

on

on any other Account than as she loves,
and the only Art she employs to
Please, is that of loving. Her Thoughts,
her Sensations had no Object but me;
always prepar'd to sacrifice to my Inter-
ests her Repose, her Happiness, and
even the very Testimony of her Tenderness. Never had any Woman a better
Way of making a Man sensible of the
Value she sets on him, the Uneasi-
nesses and Jealousies always inseparable from the Delicacy and Vivacity of a
true Affection, produce in her no Com-
plaining, no Upbraiding; her Sadness only inform'd me of her Trouble; if the
slightest Things gave Rise to it, a
Word, a Nothing, was likewise suffici-
ent to restore Joy to her, and I every
Moment tasted this Pleasure, superior to
all other, of solely constituting the De-
stiny of her I lov'd.

THE Charms, the Transports of our
Conversation are inexpressible; we
thought we had only passed some Minutes
when

when we had pafs'd many Hours; and
when we were to part, there remain'd
fo many Things to fay to each other,
that it befel us almoft always to call
one another back again, I know not
how many Times, as if we did it in
Concert. Mademoifelle *de Roye*'s Virtue
did indeed fet the moft limited Bounds
to my Defires, but the Satisfaction of
finding her more eftimable and more
worthy of my Heart, created me a
Kind of Happinefs far more fenfible to a
real Love. She fo entirely poffefs'd my
Thoughts, that whatever bore no Relation to her, was to Me infupportable.
I could yet lefs conftrain myfelf when
with Madam *de Mailly*. All my Appli-
cations were to Mademoifelle *de Mailly* ;
though fhe had no other Share in our
Confidence than that of not having defir'd to take any, I knew fhe lov'd
Mademoifelle *de Roye*, and that fhe was
belov'd by her.

MADAM

MADAM *de Mailly*, interested by the Steps which she had taken, to keep me to herself, observ'd my Behaviour not without the most violent Displeasure. The motives which commonly disunite Women, and which have so absolute a Power over those of a certain Stamp, had given her a Hatred to Mademoiselle *de Mailly*; which was still encreas'd by the Aversion Mademoiselle *de Mailly* had to a Marriage with Mr. *de Boulai*. But the Desire of Revenge silenc'd her Jealousy; she shew'd me no Signs of it, she seem'd rather by Way of Secrecy to tell me every Day a Thousand Things very capable of making an Impression on me, if I had not known Mademoiselle *de Mailly* so well as I did. I forbear to mention the Persecutions she then underwent in order to conclude her Marriage, and the Artifices which were us'd to disguise them to me.

I SAW

I SAW plainly I should never obtain Madam *de Mailly*'s Consent to marry Mademoiselle *de Roye*; she might, on the contrary, make use of the Authority she had over her, and deprive me of her for ever. Besides, how could I ask this Consent of a Woman who had discover'd to me, by Signs broad enough, that I was not indifferent to her? Without letting Mademoiselle *de Roye* into my Reasons, I resolv'd to prevail on her to comply with a secret Marriage. The greatest Obstacle which I had to surmount, was the Fear of the Wrong I might do to myself; not the least Distrust of my Word, nor of the Lot which I was preparing for her: to be united to me, was to her the chief Good, the only one which concern'd her. From the Moment she had begun to love me, a Convent had ceas'd to seem hateful to her. Whatever is not *You*, would she often say, is all alike to *Me*; even Solitude itself has the Advantage to let

me

me enjoy my Thoughts, and to help me to conceal them.

MY Meafures being taken, I got one Night into the Garden by Means of a Rope-ladder. Mademoifelle *de Roye* waited for me in this Garden, but fhe had not Strength to do more. Without giving her Time to deliberate, I re-afcended the Wall with Her in my Arms, and I led her to a little Church at a fmall Diftance, where I had procur'd a Prieft to be at Hand. I afterwards fet her down again in the Garden, after the fame Manner I had taken her out of it; and made her promife fhe would be there again the following Night. We pafs'd many more together in the fame Place. Imagine to yourfelf, if you can poffibly, what my Tranfports were. My Wife's Fondnefs, as warrantable as it was, did not fhew itfelf without a great deal of Fearfulnefs; and when I complain'd to her of it, the Occafion which I at prefent have for

your

your believing that I love you, said she
to me, deprives me of the Boldness to
tell it you, and to shew it you.

I COULD easily have carried her off
and convey'd her into *England*; but I
had no Mind she should appear there as
a Fugitive. I was sure of my Father's
Consent; but it was proper to take
Measures to get the King to approve
of my marrying a *French* Woman and
breaking off the Match which he had
made for me with Mademoiselle *Hamilton*. I was oblig'd to leave a Woman I ad-
or'd, almost the very Moment I had
begun to be happy, in order to secure to
both of us a Continuance of this Happiness.

NOTHING can express our Tenderness at Parting. I took her Twenty
Times in my Arms, she bath'd my Face
with her Tears, she conjur'd me not to
leave her. Alas! Why did I not consent

fent to it! How many Misfortunes had I
fpar'd myfelf!

MADAM *de Mailly* was furpriz'd, but
not forry for my Departure; I was a
troublefome Witnefs to the Part fhe was
acting, nay, perhaps, fhe was afraid of
fome Piece of Indifcretion from me;
for Mr. *de Boulai*, who had taken the
Impreffions of his Mother, and who
confequently was jealous of me even to
Madnefs, put my Patience every Day
to frefh Tryals.

MY Father was ftill in *Scotland*, I
went directly to him, without appearing
at Court. I was receiv'd by him in the
Manner I expected; inftead of difap-
proving my Marriage, he thought of
nothing but how to obtain the King's
Confent. The Services he had lately
perform'd in the War of *Scotland*, the
Succefs whereof was owing to his Valour and Conduct, authoriz'd him to
rely

rely on the King's Compliance. But his Services had contracted more Envy from the Courtiers, than Gratitude from the King.

EDWARD, mifled by their Artifices, perfuaded himfelf that my Marriage, which he did not believe was a Thing done, cover'd fome Defigns contrary to his Intereft, and without vouch-fafing to hear any Thing in my Behalf, order'd me to be confin'd in a clofe Prifon. Thofe to whom I was committed were ftrictly charg'd to let me fpeak with nobody, not even my Father was allow'd to fee me; and it was declar'd to me that I fhould not have my Liberty 'till I was difpos'd to fulfil the Engagements which the King had made for me.

HOWEVER fevere my Captivity was, I fuffer'd a Thoufand Times more by the Thought of what my Wife would fuffer. Alas! I fhall coft her her Life, cry'd cry'd I in thefe Difmal Moments; this is the Fruit of her Tendernefs and of her Confidence!

I HAD now pafs'd Six Months in this melancholy Manfion, when a Soldier of the Garrifon found Means to convey a Letter to me. I read it over fo often, and it made fo ftrong an Impreffion on my Heart, that not a Syllable of it has flip'd from my Memory. I will repeat the Contents to you, Word for Word:

LETTER.

WHAT have I juft now heard! You a Prifoner! This News which has penetrated even into my Solitude, has compleated Misfortunes which I fupported only becaufe I fuffer'd them Alone. Alas! our Marriage, which puts my Life and my Honour into fo great Danger, fill'd me with Joy! The Thought of my being yours for ever, put to flight all my Sorrows. But it is for me that you fuffer!

It

I

*It is I who make you unhappy! How cruel
soever this Circumstance is, it adds nothing
to my Grief. Your Misfortunes, independ-
ently of that which causes them, take up
all the Sensibility of my Heart. My Preg-
nancy, which I must acquaint you with,
will still add to your disconsolate Condition.
I was sensible of it some Time after your
Departure; and, notwithstanding the Difficulty of hiding it, I rejoyc'd at it. I see
now all the Horror of my Situation;
whom shall I trust, to assist in the Birth of
this Child, who is a Thousand Times the
dearer to me as It is yours? What shall I do
to preserve to you It and its unhappy Mother? It is for You that I desire to live!
It is for You that I fear to die! I know
Your Heart as You know Mine; you would
die for my Death. Behold the Fruit of that
Love which was to have created our
Happiness. What a Difference from those
happy Times when we were together, when
we told each other an Hundred Times in
a Moment that we lov'd each other, and
that we should always love each other! The
Remembrance of this which I incessantly*
                                    recall

*recall, increases the Load of my Afflictions.
I find myself alone in the Universe. I have
none but you, I place my Felicity in having
none but you, and I lose you. Fear nothing from me; the Shame which I shall
undergo, more terrible than the most frightful Death, shall never extort from me a
Secret, which it imports you to keep conceal'd, since you have not discover'd it.
Heaven, who knows my Innocence, who
has turn'd into a Law the softest Inclination
of my Heart, who decrees that I love you
and that I obey you, will take Pity on me
and will save my Reputation. Preserve
yourself; it is your* Amelia *who begs it of
you, bath'd in her Tears! Once more, preserve yourself; there is no other Way left
for You to shew that you love me.*

IT would be impossible for me to describe to you the Condition I found myself in after the reading of this Letter.
Pity and Honour would alone have suf-
ficed to interest me in the Fate of Madam *Arundel.* Judge then what the most
tender

tender and moſt merited Love made me feel. I cannot conceive how I was able to bear up under the Violence of my Grief; I do not believe there was ever the like. Meaſures the moſt extreme preſented themſelves to me, and if I had not been withheld by my Duty to my Wife, I had deliver'd myſelf over to them.

I WAS continually counting the Time when ſhe was to lye-in. This Time, which could not be far off, fill'd me with Terror; the moſt dreadful Images offer'd themſelves inceſſantly to me; the few Moments which my Preſſures forc'd me to give to Sleep, were diſturb'd with them; I awak'd beſide myſelf, and always drown'd in my Tears; I could do nothing in my Priſon, I could not ſo much as give the leaſt Information to my Father, who would not have abandon'd us.

K   I

I SEVERAL Times attempted to make my Efcape, but all to no Purpofe; it is true this Employment was a Kind of Mitigation to my Trouble, and the Hours which I fpent in taking afunder the Stones of the Wall, or in loofening the Iron-work of my Windows, pafs'd lefs painfully away; but the ill Succefs of my Labour threw me back into a frefh Defpair. I was fenfible I could no longer fupport the Violence of it, when the News, which came from *Scotland*, chang'd the Face of my Affairs.

THE fame Reafon of State which had made the King defirous to unite the chief Families of *England* and *Scotland*, had made the *Scots* averfe to it; they being ftill taken up with the Thoughts of fhaking off the *Englifh* Yoke. Mademoifelle *Hamilton*, who was defign'd for me, was juft married to my Lord *Barclay*, the greateft Stickler for the *Scottifh* Liberty. My Father feiz'd this
Opportunity

Opportunity to beg my Enlargement; he did not however obtain it without great Difficulty, and after engaging that I should follow the King into *France*, whither the Rupture of the Truce between the two Crowns oblig'd him to go, and that He should remain in *England*, where He should himself be confin'd 'till I had prov'd, by my Actions, that I had no Ties or Engagements contrary to the Good of the State.

As soon as I was at Liberty, my first Care was to find out the Soldier who had convey'd the Letter, and who never more appear'd. This Endeavour prov'd fruitless; I was told he was among the Troops which had been ship'd off for *France*. EDWARD embark'd soon after, and made me embark with him. It is only by your Services, said he to me, that you can wipe out the Impressions which have been given me concerning your Loyalty; expect not that I will

K 2   grant

grant you Leave to make an Alliance
with my Enemies: you muſt bring over
your Miſtreſs into the Number of my
Subjects: This is the Way to obtain
my Conſent, which I ſhall not grant to
you on any other Terms,

WE landed on the Coaſt of *Picardy*.
Iſent a Man to *Calais*, with Letters for
Madam *Arundel*; I gave him all the In-
ſtructions neceſſary for introducing himſelf into the Place. I waited his Return
with the moſt extreme Impatience. The
News he was to bring me was to decide
more than my Life; but this News ſo
much expected and ſo ardently deſir'd
came not. I ſent ſucceſſively ſeveral of
my People; not one appear'd again,
and I ſtill am ignorant what has been
their Fate.

I HAD no Hope left but in the Suc-
ceſs of the War, to which I betook
myſelf with ſo much Ardour, and, to
advance our Conqueſts, perform'd ſuch

raſh

rafh Actions and fo vifibly expos'd myfelf, that the King was forc'd to re-
ftore me to his Confidence. All my
Wifh was, that we fhould lay Siege to
Calais. The Victory which we have obtain'd has open'd us a Way to it, but
the Siege may be long : Mr. *de Vienne*
feems difpos'd to defend the Place to
the laft Extremity; and what I have
learn'd, two Days before the Battle,
does not permit me to wait the Event
of it, but obliges me to entreat a fpeedy
Affiftance from You.

A PRISONER, who had been taken
by our Men, defir'd he might be carry'd to my Tent. I knew him again
to be one *Saint-Val*, a principal dome-
ftic of Madam *de Mailly* ; I cannot tell
you how great a Difcompofure the Sight
of him gave me ; I had not the Power
to afk him any Queftions. He prevented
them, and after defiring I would difmifs
thofe who had brought him in : Some
People, Sir, faid he, have thought fit

K 3   to

to pitch upon me for their Inſtrument in a moſt deteſtable Treachery, to which I yielded, that I might be enabled to give you Notice of it. Madam *de Mailly*, underſtanding that you inclin'd to marry a Wife in *France*, and that you have thereupon thwarted the Will of EDWARD, has made no Queſtion but you have enter'd into Engagements with Mademoiſelle *de Mailly*. In order to hinder this Marriage, which ſhe cannot endure, ſhe has order'd me to get Admittance to you, under a Pretence of Services done by me to Mademoiſelle *de Mailly*, in aſſiſting to bring into the World a Child, of which I am to make You the Father; and Chance has ſo far favour'd her Wickedneſs, that ſhe can produce Proofs, which, falſe as they are, may ſeem to carry Conviction againſt Mademoiſelle *de Mailly*. The Obligation which has been laid on me to keep Secrecy, ought to give Way to that of ſuccouring oppreſs'd Innocence ; and I look upon myſelf as bound both

by

by Honour and Conſcience to unveil
this Myſtery to you.

ABOUT two Years ago, Mademoiſelle
de Roye, to whom my Mother had been
Governeſs, told me ſhe wanted to ſpeak
with me. The Condition I ſaw her in
would have ſoftned the moſt barbarous
Soul. She pour'd forth Torrents of
Tears ; it was a long Time before I
could get a Word from her: At laſt
ſhe told me, through a Thouſand Sobs,
that ſhe put her Life and Honour into
my Hands, that ſhe was with child.
Her Grief would let her ſay no more
to me, and I was ſo melted with it
that I thought of nothing but pitying
and aſſiſting her.

I CONCEIV'D it material to know the
Accomplice of her Fault; but I could
never prevail on her to own who it was.
His Name is of no Uſe, ſaid ſhe to me
ſhedding more Tears, I only am guilty.
The Favour I beg of you, is to take

K 4   Care

Care of my Child. If I dye, you will be inform'd by a Note I shall leave behind me, into what Man's Care you are to commit it.

THE Respect which I preserv'd for the Memory of my old Master, who was Mademoiselle *de Roye*'s Uncle, the Perplexity I was in, the Opinion I had conceiv'd of Madam *de Mailly*'s Prudence, the Interest she herself had to conceal this melancholy Affair, made me think I could not do any Thing better than to disclose the Matter to Her.

I HAD Room to hug myself for taking this Course. She agreed with me, that when she was near her Time, she would take Mr. *de Mailly* and Mademoiselle his Daughter to an Estate of hers in the Country; and, to avoid creating any Suspicion in the Convent, I should go as from Mademoiselle *de Roye*'s Aunt, and bring her to Mr. *de Mailly*'s, where there should

ſhould be no other Domeſtic but my
Wife and me; that my Wife, who is
a Servant of Mademoiſelle *de Mailly*,
ſhould, under ſome Pretence, aſk her
Leave to ſtay ſome Days at *Calais*.
Madam *de Mailly* farther ſaid to me,
that it was neceſſary Mademoiſelle *de*
Roye ſhould bury her Shame in the Convent, and that I ſhould diſpoſe her thereto.

MATTERS were executed in the
Manner Madam *de Mailly* had directed.
Mademoiſélle *de Roye* was brought to
Mr. *de Mailly*'s, where ſhe lay-in in the
very Chamber of Mademoiſelle *de Mailly*.
The Danger ſhe was in ſeem'd to us ſo
imminent, and my Wife was ſo unfit
to give her the proper Aſſiſtance, that
ſhe was fain to go, in the Middle of
the Night, and fetch a Woman who
profeſs'd that Buſineſs.

FROM the very Time that Mr. *Ar-*
undel had begun ſpeaking, Mr. *de Cha-*
lons,

lons, tofs'd by a Thoufand Agitations,
would have interrupted him over and o-
ver again, had not his Impatience been
check'd by the Defire he had to be
more fully enlighten'd; but being now
no longer able to contain himfelf, and
embracing Mr. *Arundel*, and fhaking
him by the Hand in the moft tender
Manner, You give me my Life a Second Time! faid he to him: What fay
I! You give me more than Life! How?
Mademoifelle *de Roye*, it feems, is your
Wife; fhe is the Mother of that Child
which has made me fo unhappy and fo
criminal. Yes, I ought to have bely'd
my Eyes; my bafe unworthy Sufpicions
deferve no Pardon, and I fhall never
forgive myfelf for them.

MR. *de Chalons* was fo overcome with
what he felt, he fpoke with fo much
Paffion, that he took no Notice of the
Surprife he had caft Mr. *Arundel* into.
I afk your Pardon, faid he to him after
his firft Tranfport, for having interrupted

ed you. Pray complete your Information; but firſt give me Leave to ſend for the Child and Woman you ſent to me. I hope they will help me to diſcharge a Part of what I owe you.

WHAT is it you put into my Head? cry'd Mr. *Arundel*; Can it be . . . . . . No; it is impoſſible. I too lightly entertain Hopes which my ill Fortune ought to have diſuſ'd me to. Fear not to entertain them, nay to give a Looſe to them, anſwer'd Mr. *de Chalons*; and whilſt they are executing the Order I have given, tell me every Thing you think I ought to know.

I AM diſabled from ſpeaking to you, reply'd Mr. *Arundel*; pity my Diſorder, vouchſafe to clear up my Doubts. It ſhall be done in a Moment, ſaid Mr. *de Chalons* ſeeing the Woman come in he had ſent for. Is Nature dumb? ſaid he taking the Child out of the Nurſe's Arms and putting it into thoſe of Mr.

K 6   *Arundel*;

Arundel; does she say nothing to you for this Child? I restore him to you, added he, with as much and more Joy than you yourself have to receive it. He then related to him how Chance had put the Child into his Power. Mr. *Arundel* listen'd to him, his Eyes all the while fasten'd on his Son, whom he press'd between his Arms and bedew'd with some Tears which Joy and Affection drew from his Eyes. I know, said he, the Features of his Mother; her Look, the amiable Sweetness of her Countenance, her Graces. This Discourse was accompany'd with a Thousand Caresses, which he incessantly lavish'd on this Son so belov'd and so happily met with. The Infant too, as if inspir'd by Nature, seem'd to know his Father; he clung to him, he was not able to leave him, he smil'd on him, he would speak to him.

MR. *de Chalons* contemplated this Spectacle with a Pleasure which the easy

eafy Situation he himfelf was in
render'd more fenfible to him. I fhould
afk your Pardon for thefe Weakneffes,
faid Mr. *Arundel* to him; but you are
too good a Man, not to be fufceptible
of the like. I know experimentally this
Moment, that the Senfations of Nature
are in no wife fhort of thofe of Love.
Alas! purfu'd he embracing his Child
again, his unhappy Mother laments the
Lofs of him. Whilft my Heart delivers
itfelf up to Joy, fhe is plung'd in the
moft frightful Defperation; fhe repents
perhaps that fhe ever lov'd me.

THE Refpect which you have for
Mademoifelle *de Mailly*, and of which
I have been inform'd, fays he to Mr.
de Chalons (after fignifying to thofe who
were prefent to void the Room) your
Refpect, I fay, for Mademoifelle *de
Mailly* demands of you the fame Things
which the Friendfhip you have for me
demands. Go fee Mademoifelle *de Mailly*
for her own Sake, for Madam *Arundel's*,
and

and for mine. Inform her of her Mother-in-law's Artifices, and what she ought to fear from her; awaken her Friendship for Madam *Arundel*, and her kind Intentions to me; prevail on her to acquaint my Wife that her Son is found, that I wait but the End of the Siege to declare my Marriage, and Never to separate myself from her. I dread left the Loss of her Son, and the Fear of being forsaken should determine her to bind herself by the *Vow*; nay, how do I know whether she will not be forc'd to it by the Malice of Madam *de Mailly*. How do I know, in short, what will be the Effect of the Grief which has so long oppress'd her! I cannot think of it without Shivering.

I AM ready to execute your Pleasure, said Mr. *de Chalons* to him who saw he had not Strength to proceed, but you are not acquainted with my last Adventures. I own, reply'd he, that what I heard of Madam *Arundel* touch'd me too

sensibly

senfibly to leave me the Liberty of putting any foreign Queftions.

Mr. *de Chalons* related to him
as briefly as he could, his Combat
with Mr. *du Boulai*, and the Confe-
quences of it. I fancy, added he, it
would be neceffary for me to talk with
Saint-Val. The Confeffion which he
made to you, proves him to have fuch
Sentiments of Probity and Honour as
may vouch for his Fidelity. So I think
too, reply'd Mr. *Arundel*, I will go and
fend him to you, and will write to Madam *Arundel* : Provided my Letter can
be convey'd to her, I am fure fhe will
do nothing againft me.

Being return'd Home, he had *Saint-
Val* conducted to Mr. *de Chalons.* Mr.
Arundel has told you who I am, faid
Mr. *de Chalons* to him, and has affur'd
you that you may place an entire Confi-
dence in me? Yes, my Lord, anfwer'd
Saint-Val ; the happy accident which has
reftor'd

reftor'd his Son to him, is an Inftance of Heaven's particular Protection of Mademoifelle *de Mailly*, whofe Innocence would have ftill been fufpected by you. Do not mention a Thing, reply'd Mr. *de Chalons*, which gives me the moft pungent Remorfe, and of which I defire you would for ever lofe the Remembrance. This Remorfe would be ftill greater, faid *Saint-Val*, if you knew all that Mademoifelle *de Mailly* has done for you. I beg you, dear *Saint-Val*, reply'd Mr. *de Chalons* in an affectionate and almoft fupplicating Manner, be fo kind as to inform me of every Thing that can have the leaft Relation to Her?

I MUST, my Lord, in order to fatisfy you, anfwer'd *Saint-Val*, recal the Time when Mr. *de Mailly* had Engagements with You. His Marriage with Madam *du Boulai* gave him other Views. But how great foever Madam *du Boulai*'s Influence was over Mr. *de Mailly*, he could not refufe Mademoifelle *de Mailly* the

the Space of Time which she desir'd to endeavour to forget You. The Marriage of Mr. *de Mailly* was perform'd all alone, and Mademoiselle *de Mailly* had for some Time no other Grievance but that of not holding any Correspondence with You.

MR. *Arundel* came to *Calais* much about that Time. What he hath been o-blig'd to own to me concerning Madam *de Mailly*'s Inclination for him, and the Jealousy which she conceiv'd against her Daughter-in-law, gives me Light into a Conduct of which, till now, I have not been able to comprehend the Motives. Mademoiselle *de Mailly* had a Thousand Persecutions to go through, to marry Mr. *du Boulai*; and they increas'd when you had carry'd off Mademoiselle *de Liancourt*.

MADEMOISELLE *de Mailly* could then no longer oppose to her Father's Will, the Inclination which she preserv-

ed

ed for You. Her Repugnance was plac'd
to Mr. *Arundel*'s Account. Mr. *du Boulai*,
infpir'd by his Mother, turn'd his whole
Jealoufy againft You; and I know not
whether he did not take you for fomebody that belong'd to him, when he
attack'd you under Mademoifelle *de
Mailly*'s Window. Your Valour deliver'd
you from thofe bafe Affaffins. Mr. *du
Boulai* knew you when you made him
deliver up his Sword, and liv'd long
enough to raife a moft violent Storm a-
gainft You and Mademoifelle *de Mailly*.

MADAM *de Mailly*, at the Sight of
her Son, all over Blood and cover'd with
Wounds, liften'd to nothing but Defpair
and Rage. It is You, faid fhe to Mr.
de Mailly, who are the Occafion of my
Misfortune. It was the Promifes which
you made me, and which you have
not had the Refolution to fulfil, that
firft kindled the Paffion of my unhappy Son; there is nothing wanting to
pierce my Heart, but to fee his Murderer

er become your Son-in-law; yes, you will have even that Weakneſs; your Daughter can do Every Thing with you, and I can do Nothing.

Mr. *de Mailly* lov'd his Wife. The Condition he ſaw her in, animated his Fondneſs. Madam *de Mailly* took Advantage of this Moment to get him to approve of her Deſigns. She ſaid you had murder'd her Son, ſhe had full Proof of it, it was neceſſary to take a Signal Revenge, it was neceſſary to make you ſuffer an ignominious Death.

How great ſoever her Aſcendant was over Mr. *de Mailly*, ſhe could not engage him in ſuch deteſtable Schemes: In Complaiſance to him, ſhe ſeem'd to lay them aſide, on Condition however that Mademoiſelle *de Mailly* ſhould marry Mr. *du Boulai* in the Condition he was in. It is abſolutely neceſſary ſaid ſhe, for her to take the Quality of his Wife, in order to ſecure me that ſhe will

never

never be his Murderer's Wife. Befides, Mr. *du Boulai* fo earneftly defir'd this Marriage, that it might perhaps have been a Means of faving his Life.

DELUDED by her Careffes and her Artifices, Mr. *de Mailly* refolved to make this ftrange Propofal to his Daughter. She anfwer'd her Father with fo much Force and Courage, and yet with fo much Refpect and Affection, that he faw himfelf oblig'd to declare the Whole to her. Madam *de Mailly*, faid fhe to him, ought to have been made eafy by the very Act of carrying off Mademoifelle *de Liancourt*, which fhe is pleas'd to make ufe of againft Mr. *de Chalons*. But if this Reafon is not fufficient for her, I give her my Word never to marry Mr. *de Chalons*; and I give it likewife to you, dear Sir, to whom nothing in the World has Power to make me break it.

THIS

THIS was not enough for Madam *de Mailly*, who dreaded You yet lefs than Mr. *Arundel*, and who wanted to gain an entire Authority over Mademoifelle *de Mailly*. She renew'd her Menaces, She infifted upon the Marriage. Mademoifelle *de Mailly* would have prefer'd Death, but fhe trembled for You; fhe knew her Father's Weaknefs, and I can't tell what might have happen'd if Mr. *du Boulai* had liv'd a little longer.

FORC'D to drop this Defign, Madam *de Mailly* form'd that with which I am charg'd. She hop'd thereby to fatisfy alike her Hatred and her Vengeance; for, my Lord, I am order'd to make all the Sufpicions of Mr. *Arundel* light on You, to excite him to meet you Sword in Hand, to engage him to make a Buftle that may lofe Mademoifelle *de Mailly* her Honour, and thereby create in you the utmoft Contempt for her.

WHAT

HORRID Scheme! cry'd out Mr. *de Chalons*: To What has not Mademoiselle *de Mailly* been expos'd! If my Life only were wanted, I would go and facrifice it to the Hatred of Her my Enemy; indeed I fhall not long preferve it, if I muft lofe all Hope. But Madam *de Mailly* hates Me much lefs than fhe hates Mademoifelle *de Mailly*; nay perhaps fhe only hates Me that fhe may have a Right to hate Her. What fhall we do, my dear *Saint-Val*? How fhall we inform Mademoifelle *de Mailly* of the flagitious Defigns which have been hatch'd againft her, and of which it is of fuch Importance for her to be inform'd? How fhall we recover her from the fatal Engagements fhe has taken againft me? How fhall we perform to Madam *Arundel* the Intentions of her Hufband?

IN Truth, my Lord, faid *Saint-Val* to him, I am very much at a Lofs; the Manner in which I have executed Ma_

dam

dam *de Mailly*'s Orders, permit me not
to shew myself at her House; besides,
it is not not possible to get into *Calais*.

MR. *de Chalons* was sensible of all
those Difficulties. *Saint-Val* had no
Motive pressing enough to surmount
them. There wanted, for that, a Passion equally warm with that which a-
ctuated Mr. *de Chalons*. After consider-
ing all Methods, he resolv'd to go to
the Count *de Canaple*, who was seeking
how to lay hold of Circumstances to
supply *Calais* with Provisions.

MR. *Arundel* agreed with Mr. *de
Chalons*, that, in order to his being more
a Master of his own Measures, the
common Opinion that he had been kill'd
in the Battle of *Cressy*, should still subsist; and he conducted him and *Saint-
Val* beyond the Lines of the Camp, from
whence they went with all the Diligence
possible to that of the *French*.

End of the Third Part.

THE

SIEGE of *CALAIS*,

BY

EDWARD of ENGLAND.

VOL. II.

FOURTH and LAST PART.

MONSIEUR *de Canaple* had been some Days departed for the Execution of a Defign he had kept to himfelf without communicating it to any Perfon whatever. This Difappointment quite drove Mr. *de Chalons* to Defpair; he attempted feveral Times to throw himfelf into *Calais*. The Defire of fucceeding

ceeding left him nothing but his Courage to confult with. He acted with fo little Caution, that he had like feveral Times to have fallen again into the Hands of the *English*. The Wounds he had receiv'd, conftrain'd him to fufpend his Enterprizes. Whilft he was, in Defpite of himfelf, confin'd to his Bed, and that his Inquietudes alfo retarded his Cure, Mr. *de Canaple* was happily executing his Project.

CALAIS, notwithftanding all Mr. *de Vienne*'s Care and Precautions, had begun to fuffer the Horrors of a moft dreadful Famine: every Thing was wanting in it, and the People of the firft Quality had in that Refpect no Manner of Privilege or Exemption. The Governor, to fet an Example of Courage and of Patience, admitted no Diftinction to be made of his own Family; nay, thofe who compos'd it were the moft expos'd to the public Calamity.

L　　THE

THE Town was block'd up on the Land Side, and the *English* Fleet hinder'd all Access to it by Sea. These Difficulties might have seem'd insurmountable to any but the Count *de Canaple*; but the Desire of performing a signal Service to his Country, and of saving the Person he lov'd, made every Thing possible to him.

THE Way of the Sea, however difficult it was, was the most practicable. He went to *Abbeville*, and found out two bold Fellows, nam'd *Marante* and *Mestriel*, who knew the Coast perfectly well, and whom the View of a Reward made blind to all Danger. The King's Coffers were exhausted; and Mr. *de Canaple* perform'd this Undertaking at the Expence of Part of his own Estate. He ship'd himself on board a Bark with these two Men, and convey'd Provisions to *Calais*.

As

As this Piece of Work was to be repeated several Times, he did not at first
go into the Town; but when he sent
these Provisions to Mr. *de Vienne*, he
order'd them to tell him that they were
principally design'd for himself and
Madam *de Granson*. He likewise desir'd that Mademoiselle *de Mailly* might
also partake thereof; the Esteem and
Friendship he had for her did not permit him to forget her.

This Supply coming at a Time when
it was so much wanted, was receiv'd by
Mr. *de Vienne* with no less Joy than
Thankfulness. He went and carry'd
this agreeable News to his Daughter:
she was still immers'd in a deep Melancholy, to which the public Calamities
would have hardly made any Addition,
had it not been out of Consideration for
her Father.

THE

THE Offence which the Count *de Canaple* had given her, the Services he had done her, the Kindnefs fhe could not help having for him, the Love fhe fufpected him to be fmitten with for Mademoifelle *de Mailly* ; all thefe different Thoughts poffefs'd her by Turns, and left her not fo much as a Moment at Eafe with herfelf. It was not however poffible that what the Count *de Canaple* had juft done fhould caufe in her no Sentiment of Pleafure, or that fhe could be infenfible of the Share fhe had in it. But this Pleafure was follow'd by a Grief mix'd with Shame, when fhe underftood that Mademoifelle *de Mailly* participated of the Succour which was given her. Her partaking of it would be no great Matter, faid fhe, but it is to Her that I owe it ; and Fortune, which perfecutes me with fo much Cruelty, expofes me to this new Mortification.

THESE

THESE Thoughts difpos'd her not to receive favourably the Count *de Canaple*; he believ'd, after having fupply'd the moft preffing Neceffities of the Town, he might tarry there fome Days. The State of Freedom which Madam *de Granfon* was in at that Time, and what he had done for her, gave him a Hope which the Warmth of his Paffion ftill increas'd, by the Neceffity which was given him of hoping. All this determin'd him to fee her, and to fpeak to her. Mr. *de Vienne* carry'd him with Eagernefs to his Daughter's Apartment.

HELP me, faid he to her, to acquit myfelf to this Heroe. Our Thankfulnefs, reply'd fhe coldly and without looking on the Count *de Canaple*, would but poorly pay the Gentleman; he expects a more glorious Return for what he has done. Mr. *de Canaple*, who was quite froze up with Madam *de Granfon*'s Reception, remain'd without anfwering a

L 3　　　　　　Word;

Word ; and being urged by an Impulfe of Refentment, he had a kind of Impatience to depart from a Place he had fo ardently wifhed to be in.

THE Deputies of the Town, who defired to wait on him, furnifhed him with a Pretence which he wanted in order to be gone, if Mr. *de Vienne*, thro' a Perfuafion that his and his Daughter's Prefence would add fomething more pleafing to the Honours that were intended him, had not ordered the Deputies to be brought in.

THE Count *de Canaple* received them with an Air of Satisfaction which he borrowed from his Refentment. It was a Revenge he exercifed againft Madam *de Granfon*, on whofe Infenfibility and Ingratitude this Publick Acknowledgment was a tacit Reflection.

A GENTLEMAN belonging to Mademoifelle *de Mailly*, who was one of the Deputies,

Deputies, had Orders to thank in particular the Count *de Canaple*. Mademoiselle *de Mailly*, my Lord, added he
when he had performed his Commiſſion,
deſires you would ſee her ſome time to-
day, if you can poſſibly. It ſhall be
this Moment, anſwered he loud enough
to be heard by Madam *de Granſon*, and
at the ſame time returning his Thanks
to the Deputies, he went out along with
them. Mr. *de Vienne* left him at Liberty
to pay a Viſit where he conceived it
might be diſagreeable to him to have
any Witneſſes; and went, according to
his Cuſtom, to inſpect the different Parts
of the Town.

MADAM *de Granſon* ſtood in need of
the Solitude ſhe was left in : She could
no longer bear the Conſtraint ſhe found
herſelf under. No ſooner was ſhe alone,
but ſhe went into her Cloſet, where ſhe
ſhut herſelf up, and caſting herſelf on a
Couch, ſhe abandoned herſelf entirely to
her Grief. All ſhe had juſt ſeen, All
L 4 ſhe

fhe had juft heard, the fatisfied Air which the Count *de Canaple* had affected, left her no Room to doubt of the Paffion fhe believed he was taken up with.

WHAT fhall I do! faid fhe. Shall I expofe myfelf to fee him come back with that Gladnefs which infults over my Shame? Shall I receive Addreffes and Refpects which he pays me only becaufe he has abufed me? The more he ftudies to make Reparation, and the more he thinks he ought to do it, he the more inftructs me in what I ought to think myfelf. Befides, how do I know whether a delicate Regard for her he loves, whether a Defire of rendering himfelf more worthy of her, is not the only Motive which makes him feek to be lefs guilty with me? Poffibly I have no other Share in his Proceedings, than to be the Sport of his falfe Virtue, after having been fo of his Caprice!

NOTWITH-

NOTWITHSTANDING this Thought, notwithstanding the Vexation it gave her, she could not forbear counting the Time which Monsieur *de Canaple* was passing with Mademoiselle *de Mailly*. Her Imagination represented to her the Pleasures of their Conversation, and made a most killing Picture of it to her. She saw Him at her Feet ; she saw Her applauding herself that the Town owed its Preservation to the Courage of her Lover, and to the Tenderness he had for her. How happy is she ! said she ; She can love, She ought to do so ; and I ought to hate ; and yet am so mean-spirited and so unhappy as to find it hard so much as to go about it ! Were he but such as when I first knew him ! Had he never injured me ! Had he loved Nothing .... But he has injured me ! But he is in love !

WHILST Madam *de Granson* was afflicting herself with the Joy and Triumphs

L 5

umphs of Mademoifelle *de Mailly*, Mr. *de Canaple* faw the Tears flow which fhe gave to Mr. *de Chalons*'s Death, and had no longer the Power to comfort her with Hopes, which at that time feemed to him abfolutely falfe. How! faid fhe to him, have I no Refource! Is it then certain that he has perifhed! Alas! could he at leaft but have known all that he hath coft me! Had he known that I renounced him, only for Himfelf! We fhould never have been Each other's, if he had lived; but he might have lived, and he would have feen I fhould never have been Another's. You are melted, faid fhe to the Count *de Canaple*, you ftill bewail a Friend you loved. You will take Comfort, added fhe, Friendfhip confoles itfelf, but I am inconfolable. My Refolution is fixed, I will go and fhut myfelf up in a Place where I may weep alone, and where I fhall be fure of Weeping eternally.

THE

THE Attachment which you have for
your Father, said the Count *de Canaple*
to her, will be a Bar to your Resolution, and makes me hope better Things
than such an Effect of your Grief. Alas!
resumed she, he has occasioned all my
Misfortune! I do not reproach him with
it; he has been weak; and is not one
always so when one loves! How do I
know what I myself might have been
capable of, if I had had a Lover less virtuous! My Heart was in his Hands.

MR. *de Canaple* admired a Way of
Thinking so reasonable, and so seldom
seen. He grieved with Mademoiselle
de Mailly for the Loss she thought she
had suffered, and he grieved too for his
own Distresses. To believe one is hated
by a Person one loves, is a Grief perhaps less supportable than to bewail their
Death.

THE

THE principal Inhabitants of *Calais* who had accompanied him, waited to conduct him to Mr. *de Vienne's*. His Return, which was a fort of Triumphal March in Miniature, was interrupted by an Inhabitant, named *Euſtache de St. Pierre*, whoſe Condition ſeemed to be not above that of a common Citizen, and who, after having made his Way through the Crowd, came and embraced the Count *de Canaple*. What, my dear Son reſtored to me! ſaid he to him, Heaven has been moved with my Tears, I ſee you once more, and ſee you the Deliverer of our Country! Was ever Father ſo fortunate, after being ſo miſerable!

THE Amazement Mr. *de Canaple* was in, who could not in the leaſt comprehend this Adventure, afforded Time to this honeſt Man, venerable for his hoary Locks, to ſurvey him more at leiſure; when proſtrating himſelf almoſt

at

at his Feet: I aſk your Pardon, my
Lord, ſaid he to him; ſo perfeƈt a
Reſemblance has occaſioned my being
guilty of this Piece of Diſreſpeƈt. I ſee
but too well, you are not my Son; I
beg you would forget my giving you a
a Name ſo unworthy of you. Alas!
this Moment has re-opened the Wounds
which Time had begun to cloſe!

THE Count *de Canaple,* touched with
his Affliƈtion, kindly raiſed him from
the Ground, and embraced him, as if
he had been indeed his Father. Do not
repent your having called me Son, ſaid
he to him; I will henceforward be as
a Son to you; Nature ſhall not in vain
have made this Reſemblance between
us: And once more embracing him, he
diſmiſſed him, and went back again to
Mr. *de Vienne's.*

MADAM *de Granſon* appeared no
more all that Day; this Continuance of
Severity made Mr. *de Canaple* quite diſtracted.

tracted. He thought it so unjust, the Services he had done so ill repaid, that there were some Moments wherein he almost repented of Every Thing he had done, and wherein he formed a Resolution to avoid the Sight of Madam *de Granson* for Ever.

WITHOUT determining what to do, he set out from *Calais*. But True Love always comes over to the Side of the Object beloved. Mr. *de Canaple* soon judged himself guilty of the Injustice with which he accused Madam *de Granson* : He found Reasons to justify her present Conduct, so different from that which she had held at *Paris*. Her Husband's Presence had tied her up to Precautions which were no longer necessary, and she might, now at Liberty, give the Reins to her Indignation. The more her Husband's Death had softened her towards him, the more she might possibly feel the Injury which had been committed against him.

As

As faft as Mr. *de Canaple's* Refentment decreafed, he re-affumed the Defire of Providing *Calais* with Supplies
againft the Dearth. That which he had
already done, engaged him to do more.
The Love of his own Fame required
from him what his Love for Madam *de
Granfon* commanded him.

THE Moments were precious. The
English might difcover their Practices,
and obftruct them. The Mariners were
ordered to get ready the little Veffels :
A furious Storm arofe juft as they were
to embark ; the two Mariners reprefented in vain to the Count *de Canaple*
the Greatnefs of the Danger ; the Storm,
inftead of difcouraging him, gave him
on the contrary a frefh Affurance of
avoiding the Enemy's Fleet.

DURING a Paffage of twenty four
Hours, they were a hundred times on
the Point of being caft away ; and when
after

after infinite Difficulties they had the
good Fortune to land at *Calais*, the
Provisions were almost all spoiled by
the Sea-water ; the Veffels wanted repairing before they could put off again.
Whilst they were at work upon them,
the King of *England*, having been informed that Provisions had been got
into the Place, ordered to be built
along the Coast little Forts to hinder
any thing going in and coming out.
It was impoffible for Mr. *de Canaple* to
purfue his Project ; being shut up in
the Town, unable for the future to
fuccour Madam *de Granfon*, no Hope
was left him but that of Dying at least
in defending her.

MR. *de Mailly*, whofe Houfe was
next the principal Attack, had defired
Mr. *de Vienne* to receive him into the
Caftle, and Mr. *de Canaple* was lodged
under the fame Roof with Mademoifelle
de Mailly. Notwithftanding Madam *de
Granfon*'s Diflike to her, it was impoffible

fible for them not to fee one another often. The Sadnefs which overwhelmed Mademoifelle *de Mailly*, fuited the Sentiment which Madam *de Granfon* had imputed to her, and confirmed her in her Opinion.

BUT this Sadnefs was always the fame, the Prefence of Mr. *de Canaple* left Mademoifelle *de Mailly* as it had found her; no Change in her, no Earneftnefs either on one Side or other to fee each other, or to feek after each other; in fhort, nothing of All that which denotes Love, and which makes it fo furely to be known. Madam *de Granfon* made all thefe Remarks, and without defigning it, fhe treated Mr. *de Canaple* the lefs ill for it; fhe however ftill avoided him with the fame Care, but not quite with the fame Difpofition.

MEAN while there was a general Dejection in *Calais:* The Braveft had

no

no longer the Heart to make ufe of a Bravery which could only defer their Deftruction a few Days ; all their Hope was in the Preparations *Philip* was making to attack the *Englifh* Camp. *Edward*, having Notice of his Defigns, added new Fortifications to his Camp.

MR. *Arundel* had Orders to march towards *Hefdin*, to obferve *Philip's* Army. It was incumbent on him to obey, however hard he found it to remove, without being informed of Madam *Arundel's* Fate, which Mr. *de Chalons*, who he thought was in *Calais*, might every Moment give him an Account of. His Son, ftill in the Hands of the Women, could not follow him ; and this Privation cut him deeply. The Care he took of this Infant, fatiffied in fome fort his Tendernefs for his Mother. To Her, were directed the Careffings he beftowed on him ; and he fancied to receive the fame from the Mother, when he received them from

her

her Child: Only he reproved himself sometimes, for relishing Pleasures which he did not share with Her.

AFTER he had placed about his Son such of his Domesticks in whom he had most Confidence, he marched at the Head of a Body of Four Thousand Men. *Philip* was set out from *Amiens*, where he had assembled his Army, and was advanced as far as *Sangate*; from whence he sent the Marshals *de St. Venant* and *de Beaujeu*, to take a View of the *English* Camp; and on their Report having judged it inattackable, he offered Battle to the King of *England*, who refused it. Having now no Means of relieving *Calais*, he saw himself forced to retire.

MR. *Arundel*, with his little Troop, fell on the Rear of the *French* Army, carried off Part of the Baggage, and took several Prisoners. This Expedition

tion being over, he refumed his Way to *Edward*'s Camp.

ONE Day, as he lay incamped in a Plain at the Entrance of a Wood, Intelligence was brought him, that fome Soldiers, allured with the Hopes of Plunder, had attempted to force a Religious Houfe, fituated in the Middle of this Wood. He immediately ran thither; his Prefence put a Stop to the Diforder, almoft as foon as it began; but it required more Time to recover the Nuns again from their Fright, whom the Cuftom of living in a Solitude and in Retirement ftill rendered more fufceptible of Fear.

THE Gate of the Houfe, which had been forced, gave Mr. *Arundel* Liberty to enter in. The Nuns, zealous to teftify their Gratitude to him, led him into a very fpacious Inclofure, which fupplied them with Suftinence, and likewife

wife ferved them to walk and take the
Air in.

PASSING over a little ruftick
Bridge which was laid crofs a Brook,
he faw on that Side he was going to,
a Perfon fitting on a Stone, fo deeply
penfive, that fhe was not aware any body
was coming towards her, till they were
near her. Without looking at thofe
who were advancing, fhe got up to be
gone. But Mr. *Arundel* had fufficiently
feen her, to go up to her and take her
in his Arms, with the warmeft Tranfports of Love.

KNOW me again, my dear *Amelia*,
faid he to her; look at him you
fhun: It is I, it is a Hufband who ad-
ores you, whom the Lofs of you has almoft killed with Grief. The Surprize,
the Emotion, the Joy of Madam *Arundel*
had like to have coft her her Life. She
remained fenfelefs in the Arms of her
Hufband.

A T

A t the Sight of this Accident, Mr. *Arundel*, feized with Fear, and quite befide himfelf, defired Affiftance of All about him. He placed his Wife on the Brook-fide, he caft Water on her Face, he defired her in the moft tender Terms to anfwer him; but all his Endeavours were ineffectual, fhe could not be brought to herfelf.

T h e y carried her to a little Houfe belonging to the Gardener, near at hand. After having employed all the Remedies that could be thought on, fhe gave fome Sign of Life; her Eyes opened themfelves fome time after, and looked about for Mr. *Arundel*. He was on his Knees by her Side, his Mouth glued to one of her Hands. Madam *Arundel* looked on him fome time, and cafting round his Neck the Arm which was left unengaged, fhe continued in this Situation.

T h e

THE Diforder wherein they both were, fuffered them not foon to fpeak; their Looks were blended together, and faid to each other what their Tongues could not utter. Madam *Arundel* took her Hufband's Hands, and kiffed them, in Her turn. To thefe firft Moments fucceeded a Thoufand Queftions, always interrupted by new Teftimonies of Tendernefs.

IT was neceffary to think of conveying Madam *Arundel* to a Place where fhe might pafs the Night with lefs Inconveniency: She might have gone into the Convent, but Mr. *Arundel* could not follow her there; and how could he leave her? He fent in all hafte for a Chariot, to carry her to an adjoining Village. All the Way, as fhe went, bufied with a Thoufand Cares of which fhe was the fole Object, he walked by the Side of the Chariot.

MADAM

MADAM *Arundel,* whom they put to Bed as foon as they reached the Place, feemed better at firft, but was feized that Night with a Fever, which increafed the following Days. The Defire of affifting her fupported Mr. *Arundel's* Spirits, and prevented his finking under the Weight of his Affliction; his Eyes always faftened on her, always in the moft exquifite Emotion of Fear and Hope, he would never leave her Bed-fide. The Fever grew confiderably more violent, and the fick Lady gave no Hope of Recovery.

THERE was no concealing her Condition from Mr. *Arundel*; more dead than alive, overpowered with Tears and Sobs which he endeavoured to ftifle, he would, to alleviate the Pain which Madam *Arundel* felt in her Head, reach his Hand to the Place; fhe took this Hand, kiffed it, and put it to her Forehead.

SOME

SOME Moments after, perceiving that
Mr. *Arundel* wept, and would conceal
it; Let me see your Tears, said she to
him, raising herself up a little, and
looking on him with Eyes which, tho'
dying, still retained their Beauty: let
me enjoy the Pleasure of being so perfectly beloved. Alas! I fear I have but
a few Moments more to enjoy it; Death
is going perhaps to part us this Minute.
My Tears flow no less than yours, continued she. Life is very dear, when
one is held to it by the strongest Ties of
Love! No, cried Mr. *Arundel*, Heaven
will have Pity on me; you will not die,
or I shall die with you.

IF I could, replied Madam *Arundel*,
put into your Arms a Son we had, I
should die with less Regret; but, notwithstanding all my Endeavours and all
my Entreaties, he was snatched from me,
and we have lost him for Ever. No, my
dear *Amelia*, he is not lost; you would

M have

have had him already with you, if I had not feared giving you too great an Emotion. You do not know, said she to him, looking on him in the most affectionate manner, how much you are beloved; my Son, without You, would be Every thing to me ; with You, he is but my Son. If it is possible, give me the Confolation to embrace him.

MR. *Arundel*, who had taken Care to send for his Son as soon as he had found Madam *Arundel* again, ordered him to be fetched. She found herself, when she saw him, more affected than she thought she should be. She would have him near her ; she never ceased hugging him. You have occasioned me many Misfortunes, said she to him embracing him, but I do not love you the less for it. Why should not I love him ? added she, directing her Speech to Mr. *Arundel*, it is our Son, it is one Tye the more which unites us.

WHETHER

WHETHER it was the Joy that had wrought a sudden Revolution on Madam *Arundel*, or that her Malady was at its last Period, she found herself considerably better that very Night: And the Fever quite left her a few Days after. It was not till then that Mr. *Arundel* related to her what he had been told by *Saint-Val*, and the almost miraculous Manner in which their Son had been found again. But, added he, What Methods have been taken to keep you so entirely in the dark as to what was doing in your native Place?

You know, answered she, that I was sent back to the Convent, immediately after I had lain-in: All Converse was forbid me; all Correspondence was cut off from me. *Saint-Val*, charged by Madam *de Mailly* to order me to take the Veil, was the Only Person I had Liberty to speak to; my Health was so bad, that the Nuns themselves declared

M 2 they

they could not receive me till I was re-covered. In this manner I lived, sup-ported by the sole Confidence I had in You, when Madam *de Mailly*, whom for a long time I had heard nothing of, entered my Chamber.

A CHARIOT, said she to me in a sharp menacing Tone, waits for you at the Gate, and has Orders to carry you to a House which I have pitched upon for you. Be gone this Instant, and thank me for taking you from a Place where your Shame might not always be con-cealed. You know my timorous Tem-per, pursued Madam *Arundel* ; besides, what could I have done to ward off the Blow? I could do nothing but Obey.

THEY took from me in general All I had, lest I might make any Use thereof for my Relief. By good Fortune, your Letters and your Picture, which I always kept concealed about me, were left me,

and

and have been my Only Confolation in
my Solitude.

A Woman and a Man whom I knew
not, ftayed for me in the Chariot. I
was carried and watched all the Way,
with as much Circumfpection as if I had
been a Prifoner of State. My Modera-
tion and my Complaifance could gain
nothing upon my Conductors Minds :
they ufed me with fo much Inhumanity,
that it was a kind of Relief to me, when
I found myfelf in the Houfe where you
faw me. But when I was informed of
the Rule which was obferved therein,
when I underftood that they lived in an
abfolute Forgetfulnefs of the World,
that I fhould never hear any body fpoke
of, nor any body ever hear Me fpoken
of, I thought I was in the Grave.

Even the Death of their neareft Relations is never made known to thefe Good
Maidens but in General Terms. How
many Tears has this fort of News caufed
me

me to fhed, though it could no ways regard You! It filled my Mind with the
moft difmal Ideas. The Ignorance I was
in, and wherein I was like to continue for
ever of Your Fate, created me continual
Alarms.

I HAD no other Profpect of the
Conclufion of my Sufferings but that of
my Life, and yet I would not *engage*
myfelf. That had been Ceafing to be
Yours; that had been depriving me of
the Name of your Wife. This Name,
though none but myfelf knew it belong'd
to me, yet comforted me.

I WENT almoft every Day to mufe in
the Place where you found me. The
Solitude and Silence increafed my Me-
lancholy; I filled my Heart with it, I
read over your Letters again and again;
I looked on your Picture, and I wept.
My Health, which grew weaker every
Day, gave me Hopes of an approaching
Death.

MADAM

MADAM *Arundel*, melted with such doleful Remembrances, had not Power to say any more. Mr. *Arundel*, pierced to the Heart, repeated to her what he had a Thousand times told her, that his Blood, his Life could not repay the leaft of the Troubles fhe had fuffered for Him.

HE could not prevail with himfelf to leave her. But She, always concerned for her Hufband's Intereft and Reputation, obliged him to return to the Siege of *Calais*, whither he had fent back the Troops under the Command of the Earl of *Northampton*. What did he not fay to her at parting! How many Precautions taken, how many Methods of hearing from her! He would be informed every Moment of her Welfare.

THE King of *England* ordered him at his Arrival, to go with Mr. *de Mauny*, and talk with Mr. *de Vienne*, who, from

M 4   the

the Top of the Walls, had notified by
a Signal, that he had Something to say.
Philip's Retreat leaving this brave Com-
mander no farther Hope of Succour, he
had not been able to refuse to the Inhabitants of the Town, and to the Gar-
rison, the Demand of a Capitulation.

My Lords, said he to my Lord *Arundel* and Mr. *de Mauny*, the King my
Master has committed this Place to My
Trust; it is near a Year you have
been besieging me in it: I have done
my Duty, as well as Those who are
shut up with me. Scarcity of Provisions, and the Want of Succours constrain us to surrender; but we will
bury ourselves under the Ruins of
these Walls, unless such Conditions be
granted us as may secure our Lives, our
Liberties, and our Honour.

Mr. *de Mauny*, instructed in the Intentions of *Edward*, and more disposed
by his Character than Mr. *Arundel*, to
discharge

difcharge the Commiffion which he had
fent them upon, declared that the King
would admit them to no Compofition ;
that they fhould be entirely at His Mer-
cy, and undergo what Punifhment He
fhould think proper to inflict upon them.
Mr. *de Vienne* anfwered with much Refolution, that the Inhabitants and Himfelf could die with their Swords in their
Hands ; but that he believed the King
of .*England* to be too Prudent and too
Generous to reduce brave Men to Defpair.

RETURNING to the Camp, Mr.
Arundel and Mr. *de Mauny* left no Method untried to foften their Mafter's
Wrath ; they reprefented to him in the
ftrongeft Manner, that the Severity
which he fhould ufe to the Befieged,
might prove of dangerous Confequence,
and give *Philip* a Right to imitate him.
I will, faid *Edward* to them, after ftu-
dying fome time, grant the Governor
the Favour he afks, on Condition that

M 5 SIX

Six Citizens, Natives of *Calais*, shall be delivered up to Me with a Rope about each of their Necks, to perish by the Hands of the Common Hangman. It is necessary their Punishment should deter other Cities which, after the Example of this, might incline to resist me. Mr. *Arundel* and Mr. *de Mauny* were forced to carry this terrible Answer to Mr. *de Vienne*.

BEFORE he assembled the People, he went to Madam *de Granson*'s Apartment, followed by the Count *de Canaple*, whom he had desired to accompany him. We must for ever be separated from each other, my dear Daughter, said he to her, embracing her; I am going to lay before the People *Edward*'s Answer, and for want of the Six Victims which he demands, and which I cannot give him, I will go and offer him my own Head; perhaps he will suffer himself to be wrought upon; perhaps I shall prevent the Misfortune of this City and of You.
My

My Death will at leaſt ſave me the Shame and the Grief of being Witneſs to it. If I am accepted of, your Retreat is free; and if I periſh without ſaving You, I entreat Mr. *de Canaple,* whoſe Valour I know, to uſe all Means to preſerve You from the Fury of the Conqueror. I hope that by the Advantage of the Tumult and Diſorder, it will not be impoſſible for you to get off ſafe in ſome Fiſhing-boat.

How! Father, cried Madam *de Granſon,* claſping him in her Arms, and bedewing him with her Tears, will You die, and do you take Meaſures to ſave My Life! Do you then believe that I will or that I can ſurvive You? The Moment you go out of this unhappy City, ſhall be the Moment of my Death.

The Count *de Canaple,* no leſs pene-trated than Mr. *de Vienne* and Madam *de Granſon,* looked on them both, and

M 6   kept

kept Silence, when Madam *de Granson,* lifting up her Eyes on him swollen with Tears : Take care of Yourself, Sir, said she to him ; I need no other Assistance but my Despair. No, Madam, said he to her, you shall not have Recourse to so terrible a Remedy ; and if Mr. *de Vienne* will please to put off the Assembly till To-morrow, I entertain great Hopes from a Contrivance I have just been thinking of.

MR. *de Vienne,* though thoroughly persuaded of Mr. *de Canaple's* Courage and Capacity, yet did not promise himself any Success therefrom. Madam *de Granson,* on the contrary, gave way to some Hope.

MR. *de Canaple* went, after he had left them, to *Eustache de Saint-Pierre,* the same who had taken him for his Son. I am come, said he to him, to desire you would own me for that Son whom you thought me so greatly to resemble.
I have

I have Occasion for that Name, in order to be accepted by the Deputies of *Edward*, who will have Six Citizens of *Calais* to be delivered up to him, and who will not pardon the rest of the City but upon that Condition.

EUSTACHE had a Firmness of Soul, an Elevation of Spirit and Mind far above his Birth, and rarely to be met with even in the most exalted Stations of Life. The Honour which you do me, my Lord, said he to the Count *de Canaple*, teaches me what I ought to do myself. I will shew, if I can, that I am worthy to have such a Son as You: we will go together and offer ourselves for the first Victims.

NEXT Day the People were convened by Mr. *de Vienne*; nothing was heard but Cries, but Groanings throughout this consternated Multitude; the Certainty of inevitable Death, whatever Course they took, gave no body the
Courage

Courage to die, at leaſt beneficially for their Country.

H o w ! ſaid then *Euſtache de Saint-Pierre* ſhewing himſelf to the Aſſembly, this Death which we have Dared for a Year paſt, is it become more formidable To-day? What then is our Hope? Shall we eſcape the Barbarity of the Conqueror? No. We ſhall die, and we ſhall die ſhamefully, after we have ſeen our Wives and our Children delivered over to Death, or to the laſt of Ignominies.

T H E Horror which the Aſſembly was full of, redoubled this frightful Picture. *Euſtache*, interrupted by more Cries and freſh Groanings, at length proceeded : But why theſe vain Diſcourſes, when 'tis Examples are wanted? I give, for the Safety of my Fellow-Citizens, my own Life and that of my Son. Though he is not here with
me,

me, he will meet us at the City-Gate.

WHATEVER Admiration was raifed in each Breaft by *Euftache's* Virtue, it feemed as if Heaven, to reward him, was pleafed that his Family Alone fhould furnifh out Examples of Courage. *John d'Aire*, *James de Wuifant*, and *Peter* his Brother, all near Relations to *Euftache*, prefented themfelves.

THE Number was not yet complete. Mr. *de Vienne*, to be admitted therein, ufed the fame Endeavours as others would have done to exempt themfelves from it. But the Deputies, full of Refpect and Veneration for fo Heroic a Virtue, inftead of liftening to him, ftuck to *Edward's* Commands, and declared they could not alter them in the leaft.

MADAM

MADAM *de Granson*, being inform'd of all that pass'd, saw nothing but Destruction; there was no Way but by performing the impos'd Conditions, to save the Life of a Father who was dear to her; there was no other Price but this, by which she could save herself from the Rage of the victorious Soldier. What was Mr. *de Canaple* doing? What were become of the Hopes he had given? Why did he not appear? Has he left off to be generous? This Misfortune was wanting to me, said she: to finish my Shame, it was necessary he should be even unworthy of the Esteem I had for him, that Esteem which I condemn'd myself for having, and which, however, I was very glad to owe him.

MADEMOISELLE *de Mailly*, who, from the Time she had been lodg'd in the Castle, was accustom'd to the Sight of Madam *de Granson*, came and griev'd with her. Death was not what she fear'd; since she had lost Mr. *de Chalons*, she
look'd

look'd on That as a Blessing ; Misfortunes a Thousand Times greater than Death made her Tears flow.

A LOUD Noise which she heard, interrupted this sad Employment : as every Thing was to be fear'd in the present Situation, they hasten'd to a Window which look'd into the Square ; they saw at first nothing but a great Multitude of People assembled together, and heard nothing but a confus'd Noise. But as the Objects drew nearer, they distinguish'd Five Men with a Rope about each of their Necks ; the Crowd follow'd them, all were desirous to see them, all were desirous of bidding a last Farewel ; the Whole rung with their Praises, and the Whole was in Tears. Madam *de Granson* and Mademoiselle *de Mailly* were struck through with so moving a Spectacle ; the Pity which these unfortunate Persons inspir'd them with, was increas'd by the Constancy

and

and Courage with which they went to their Death.

ONE amongst them, in spite of the sad Condition he was in, was distinguish-able by his good Mien, by a more ma-jestic and more resolute Deportment, and engag'd every body's particular Notice. Hardly had Mademoiselle *de Mailly* plac'd her Eye on him, but, sending forth a loud Shriek, she fell in-to a Swoon.

MADAM *de Granson,* astonish'd and surpriz'd at this Accident which she could not tell what to ascribe to, call'd out for Help. They carried Mademoiselle *de Mailly* to her Bed, where she continu'd a long Time with-out any Sense; at last she open'd her Eyes, and pushing away those who were going to relieve her; let me alone, said she, let me die, it is prolonging my Sufferings to prolong my Life; Heavens! added she, what have I just seen? He

lives

lives, and his Life renders my Grief more bitter; is then his Life given him only to lose it by the Hand of an Executioner!

I BEG your Pardon, Father, said she to Mr. *de Mailly*, who ran in at the Noise of this Accident; I beg your Pardon for alarming you thus with my Sorrow, but can you condemn it? This *Chalons* whom you allow'd me to love, whom you design'd me for, whom you took away from me, is going to perish for You and for Me. I have seen him, I knew him again; he is already, this dreadful Moment, in the Power of the Barbarian! Why cannot he know that my Death will follow his! Do not lament me, Father, let me die without having offended you; how know I Whither the Excess of my Grief may lead me? A second Fit which then seiz'd her, much stronger than the first, fill'd them all with Apprehensions of her expiring. Mr. *de Mailly* clasp'd his Daughter in

hi

his Arms, and look'd as if he himfelf
was going to expire too.

MADAM *de Granfon*, whofe Sufpicions were by this Time much diminifh'd,
being fully enlighten'd by what fhe
heard, felt her Friendfhip for Mademoifelle *de Mailly* fpring up again in her
Heart, in Proportion as Jealoufy de-
creas'd in it; and notwithftanding the
piteous State fhe faw her in, fhe envy'd
her. She is belov'd, faid fhe, fhe has
dar'd to love, fhe receives from Him
fhe loves the greateft Proof of Love
which any one can receive; and here
am I who have receiv'd nothing but In-
dignities, nothing but Outrages: Such
is the Reward of my Weaknefs.

MR. *de Vienne*, who did not appear,
gave Madam *de Granfon* a frefh Affliction. She went from Mademoifelle *de
Mailly* to look for her Father, when fhe
was inform'd by a Man belonging to
him, that he was in hoftage in the
Hands

Hands of my Lord *Montaigu*, and
that he was not to be set free 'till the
Citizens, on whom *Edward* resolv'd to
exercise his Vengeance, should have
suffer'd the Punishment they were condemn'd to.

A GENTLEMAN of the Horse to the
Count *de Canaple* put into her Hands at
the same Time a Letter he was charg'd
with. The Consternation He seem'd to
be in, threw Her too into the most terrible Apprehensions. She took and o-
pen'd the Letter with a trembling Hand,
and read what follows with a Disorder
which encreas'd at every Line.

LETTER.

*NOT 'till this Moment, wherein I am
going to my Death, have I ever dar'd
to tell you I love you. You have not been
ignorant of it, Madam; your Rigours,
your Severities have long since inform'd me
as much; but have you known what this*

3   *Passion*

Paſſion is which you have inſpir'd me with?
Have you conceiv'd that my Heart aſk'd
nothing, deſir'd nothing but yours; that it
was in your Power with a Word, with a
Look to make my Happineſs? This, Ma-
dam, is the Man whom you have loaded
with ſo much Hatred. I have never per-
mitted myſelf to ſpeak to you; I have laid
myſelf under Laws full as ſevere as any you
yourſelf could have laid me under; I have
made myſelf as wretched as you was willing
I ſhould be. I had hop'd that ſo ſubmiſ-
ſive a Behaviour would at laſt have taught
you, that Fortune alone had been able to
make me criminal. I will farther own to
you, Madam, I ſometimes flatter'd myſelf
that Decency and Duty were more againſt
me than you was yourſelf. You have taken
from me this Illuſion which was ſo dear to
me, which kept me alive. The Change of
your Condition has made mine yet more mi-
ſerable. You have ſhun'd me, You have
rejeẛed my Services with a new Rigour;
no Hope is left me: there is a Neceſſity to
put an End to ſo many Sufferings; I muſt
ceaſe

*cease to be odious to you, by ceasing to live.
I shall carry off at least the Consolation of
having given you, to the latest Moment,
Marks of that exquisite Respect which
hath always accompanied my Love. It is
under a fictitious Name that I offer myself to Death. You alone will be acquainted with my Fate; you alone, Madam, of
the whole World, will know that I die
for you.*

WHAT Sentiments! What Tenderness did not the Reading of this Letter
produce in her! This Man, for whom
Madam *de Granson* had, from the very
first Moment, so natural an Inclination,
by whom she had not believ'd she was
belov'd, gave his Life to save hers!
This Man had the most sincere, and the
the most pleasing Passion! The Joy of
being so perfectly belov'd made its Way
to her very Heart, through Grief and
Pity. The more Mr. *de Canaple* thought
he was hated, the more she thought him
worthy of her Love. Every Thing seem'd
posible

poffible to her; every Thing feem'd lawful to her to fnatch him from Death.

Go, I befeech you, go, faid fhe to him who had brought her the Letter; fetch me a Man's Habit, and prepare to follow me to the Camp. The Life of your Mafter, perhaps, depends upon your Diligence. During the fhort Space 'till the Man return'd, Mr. *de Canaple*, expiring under the Executioner's Hands, prefented himfelf without ceafing to Madam *de Granfon*'s Eyes, and made her almoft die every Inftant.

THE Detention of Mr. *de Vienne* gave her the Liberty of going out of the Town without Obftruction. Notwithftanding her natural Delicacy, fhe walk'd with fo much Speed that fhe left far behind her the Perfon fhe had taken for a Guide; but her Diligence was too flow for her Impatience: fhe chid herfelf for wanting Strength, fhe trembled left fhe fhould not arrive foon enough.

WHEN

WHEN she had reach'd the foremost Guard, a Soldier, deceiv'd by her Clothes, took her for a Man, and was for stopping her; but an Officer, moved by her Aspect, took her from the Soldier, and led her to the Tent of the King, to whom she aver'd she had an important Secret to reveal.

SIRE, said she to him falling on her Knees before him, I come to beg Death of you; I come to offer you a guilty Head, and to save an innocent one. I was of the Number of those Citizens who are to perish for the Safety of All; a Stranger, through an Effect of Pity injurious to Me would rob Me of this Glory, and has assum'd My Name.

EDWARD, with all the Qualities which constitute the Heroe, was not exempt from the Weaknesses of Pride. The Proceedure of Madam *ae Granson*, by setting before him the Cruelty which

N   he

he had given Way to, provok'd him ſtill more highly; and looking on her with Eyes full of Anger, Did you think, ſaid he to her, you could diſarm my Vengeance by coming to out-brave it? You ſhall die, ſince you have a Mind to die; and this audacious Perſon who has dared to deceive me, ſhall die with you.

AH! Sire, cry'd Madam *de Granſon,* command, at leaſt, that I die firſt; and dragging herſelf to the Knees of the Queen, who that Moment came into the King's Tent, Ah! Madam, have Pity on me, obtain this ſmall Favour. Am I ſo guilty to be condemn'd to the moſt cruel Puniſhment, to ſee Him die who dies only to ſave Me!

HER Firmneſs forſook her in pronouncing theſe Words, and ſhe could not refrain ſhedding ſome Tears. The Queen, already touched with the Fate of theſe unhappy Perſons, and who came

came with the Defign of obtaining their
Pardon, was yet more foftned by the
Speech and Action of Madam *de Granfon*, and declar'd herfelf abfolutely in
their Favour.   The Glory fhe had acquir'd by winning feveral Battles, and
by taking the King of *Scotland* *, had
given her a Right to afk Any Thing ;
but EDWARD, ftill inflexible, made no
Anfwer but by commanding an Officer
of his Guards to haften the Execution of
the Prifoners.

THIS Command, which left Madam
de Granfon without farther Hope, awaken'd all her Courage.   Rifing from her
Knees, in which Pofture fhe ftill was
before the Queen, and looking upon
EDWARD with a Pride mix'd with Indignation : Difpatch then, faid fhe to

---

* *Bruce*, King of *Scotland*, had made an Ir-
ruption into *England*, whilft EDWARD was in
France. He was defeated and taken by the Queen
of *England*, who put herfelf at the head of fom :
Troops which fhe had got together in Hafte.

him

him, haften the fulfilling your Word, and let me be led to Death. But know you are going to fpill the Blood of One, eminent enough to find Avengers.

GREATNESS of Soul has Privileges o-ver the Hearts of Heroes, which it never lofes. EDWARD, in fpite of his Anger, could not refufe his Admiration to Ma-dam *de Granfon*. Being more moved at the Firmnefs with which fhe perfifted to afk for Death, than he had been with her Sorrow ; and thefe laft Words of hers, making him fufpect fomething Extraordinary in this Adventure which deferved to be examined into, he made a Sign to thofe who were in his Tent, to withdraw. Your Life, faid he then to her, and that of your Fellow-Citizens will depend on your Sincerity. What powerful Motive is it that has determined you to act as you do?

I COULD much more eafily die, Sir, replied fhe, than make the Confeffion
you

you exact of me; but the Concern of a
Life far more dear than my own, triumphs over my Reluctance. You see at
your Feet a Woman, who has been Weak
enough to love, and who has had Strength
enough to conceal that she loved. My
Lover, persuaded that he was hated, had
yet Generosity and Passion enough, to sacrifice his own Life to the Preservation of
mine. An Action so tender, so generous, has made on my Heart its whole
Impression. I have believed in My turn
that I owed Him the same Sacrifice; and
my Gratitude and my Love have brought
me hither.

But, said the Queen, why so much
of Constraint? For I suppose you are
Free, and that your Inclination is lawful. I have not always been Free, Madam, answered she; and since the Time
I have been so, it required an Action
extraordinary as this is to extort from
me a Confession of my Weakness.

N 3   WEO

WHO then is this Man, resumed EDWARD, who has done so much for you? and Who are You Yourself? My Procedure, Sire, answered she with a Countenance which shewed her Confusion, should make me hide my Name for ever. I must however own, that it puts me to less Pain to tell Your Majesty I am Daughter to the Governor of *Calais*, than to name Mr. *de Canaple*.

EDWARD could hold out no longer. Enforced by his own Affections, and determined by the Instances the Queen made, he ordered Mr. *Arundel* and Mr. *de Mauny*, whom he sent for in, to go fetch the Prisoners to him. These two Lords made haste to execute an Order which they received with so much Pleasure.

Two of the Six, already on the Scaffold, beheld without any Alteration the Preparatives of their Execution; and though they embraced each other tenderly

derly, yet it was without any Weaknefs. Mr. *Arundel*, who faw them afar off, cried, Pardon! Pardon! he made towards them with all Expedition, and, to his great Surprize, found one of them to be Mr. *de Chalons*.

SHALL I believe my Eyes? faid he to him embracing him. Is it You I fee? Is it Mr. *de Chalons* I have fnatched from the Hands of the Executioner? By what ftrange Chance is fuch a Man as You found here? I am not here alone, anfwered Mr. *de Chalons*; Mr. *de Canaple*, whom you fee, has done what I have done, and what you yourfelf would have done in our Circumftances.

MR. *Arundel*, at the naming of Mr. *de Canaple*, faluted him with all the Marks of Refpect. Let us haften, faid he to them, from a Place whither I blufh for my Nation that you could be led, and come to the King, to whom we are commanded to bring you.

MR.

Mr. *de Chalons* told him as they went, that it was but two Days since he could get into *Calais*. Pardon me, my Lord, that I have not fulfilled your Intentions, and that I have thought only how to save Mademoiselle *de Mailly* in this Juncture. I have nothing now to ask of your Friendship, replied Mr. *Arunael:* I am re-united to Madam *Arundel*; I have no Wishes to make but for Your Happiness; and turning to Mr. *de Canaple*, I should be very glad too, said he to him, if I could contribute to Yours. Mr. *de Chalons* will be so good as to assure you that you may rely upon Me.

They were now so near the King's Tent, that Mr. *de Canaple* had scarce Time to thank him for such obliging Offers. Mr. *Arundel* went in and informed the King of his Prisoners Names.

Madam *de Granson* no sooner heard Mr. *de Canaple* named, but casting herself again at the Queen's Feet: Ah! Madam,

Madam, faid fhe to her, grant me the Favour to withdraw myfelf; I cannot fupport the Shame which oppreffes me, and the Indecency of the Habit I am in. How? anfwered the Queen, who had obferved her Diforder at the Mention of Mr. *de Canaple*'s Name, Do you fear the Sight of a Man for whom you have defired to die?

THE Sacrifice of Life, Madam, replied fhe, is not always the moft difficult. Your Sentiments are fo honourable, faid the Queen, that they infpire me with no lefs Efteem for you than they at firft infpired me with Pity. I am defirous you fhould be happy, and do promife you to ufe my Endeavours to make you fo. Go, follow my Lady *Warwick*; fhe will take care to give you the Things which are neceffary for you.

I PRESUME, Madam, to afk your Majefty another Favour, replied Madam *de Granfon*. My Father is bewailing

N 5 thofe

thofe whom Your Goodnefs has faved: vouchfafe to order fomebody to go and dry up his Tears. You fhall be fatisfied, faid the Queen, difmiffing her.

MR. *de Canaple* and Mr. *de Chalons* were afterwards introduced. I did not believe, faid the King to them, that I had faved the Lives of fuch dangerous Enemies. I know that the Courage of ye Both have more than once retarded my Victories. Be pleafed, Sire, anfwered Mr. *de Canaple*, not to recall Things which Your Majefty's Goodnefs might make us repent of, if it were poffible for us to repent of having done our Duty. Peradventure, faid EDWARD to him fmiling, I could put your Virtue to more dangerous Trials. Go with Lord *Arundel* to Lord *Warwick*, and return your Thanks to the Perfon to whom you really owe your Life.

THE Count *de Canaple*, to whom it was not permitted to afk the King Queftions

ftions, was no fooner out of his Prefence,
but he afked my Lord *Arundel*, with an
Impatience and a Diforder of which he
could not divine the Caufe, what it was
the King meant. All I know, faid Mr.
Arundel to him, is, that a young Man
of exquifite Beauty, whom I juft now faw
at the Queen's Feet, is come to beg of
the King to die in Your ftead. Ah! my
Lord, cried out the Count *de Canaple*,
who durft not believe what came into his
Mind, I fhall die if you have not the
Goodnefs to fatisfy my Impatience. You
will not be long in Sufpenfe, faid my
Lord *Arundel* to him, we are got to my
Lady *Warwick*'s, where I was ordered to
carry you, and where I leave you.

MADAM *de Granfon* was alone with a
Woman whom my Lady *Warwick* had
given her to wait on her, when Mr. *de
Canaple* came in. What! Madam, cried
he out, running haftily to her, and cafting
himfelf at her Feet, is it You! is it You,
Madam! The whole Univerfe were not
worthy of what You have done!

MADAM

MADAM *de Granfon*, a thoufand times more abafhed and confounded than ever fhe had been, turn'd her Eyes down, kept Silence, and endeavoured to convey herfelf away from the fervent Addreffes of the Count *de Canaple*. Vouchfafe to look on me a Moment, Madam, faid he to her; why did you fave my Life, if your Will is that I fhould be ftill wretched?·

SINCE it was neceffary Somebody fhould die to fave my Father, faid fhe at laft, it was incumbent on Me to die. Ah! Madam, anfwered he, ftruck thro' with Grief, what Apprehenfions do you fill me with! It is Duty alone has brought you then hither! And how could I a Moment think otherwife? You was then lefs reluctant to part with Life, than to owe any thing to My Memory! You do not think fo, faid Madam *de Granfon*, looking on him with Eyes full of an Indulgent Softnefs, and perhaps I ought to juftify myfelf to you for what I have done for you.

JUSTIFY

JUSTIFY yourſelf! You, Madam·! replied Mr. *de Canaple* with much Warmth.. Pray, let us put an end to this Converſation, ſaid ſhe to him, your Complaints would be unjuſt, and your Acknowledgments give me too much Confuſion. What Reſtraints do you lay me under, Madam? replied Mr. *de Canaple* ; read what you will not hear, and what I could ſpeak with ſo much Pleaſure.

MR. *de Chalons*, eager to ſee Madam *de Granſon* to hear News of Mademoiſelle *de Mailly*, entered the Room at this ſame time along with Mr. *Arundel*. Madam *de Granſon*'s firſt Intention was to get up and be gone. She could not reconcile herſelf to what ſhe had done, and would gladly have been concealed from all Eyes ; but Mr. *de Chalons* begged her ſo earneſtly to ſtay, that ſhe was forced to conſent to it. To excuſe perhaps the Step ſhe had taken, ſhe began to relate to him the Sorrow of Mademoiſelle *de Mailly*,

Mailly, when she had found it was him.

THE Pleasure of being beloved, how-great soever, is not greater than our Concern for what we love. Mr. *de Chalons* saw nothing, felt nothing, but the Affliction of Mademoiselle *de Mailly*. He prayed Madam *de Granson*, not to defer a Moment her Return to *Calais*. She would with Pleasure have yielded to his Request, but it was necessary to get the Queen's Leave. Mr. *Arundel*, secure of that Princess's Goodness, took upon him to obtain it.

WHILST he was gone to ask it, Mr *de Chalons* gave Madam *de Granson* an Account of every thing that concerned him, and told her the Reasons which had engaged Mr. *de Canaple* to visit Mademoiselle *de Mailly* with such Assiduity. Madam *de Granson* could have no Remains of Doubt upon her Mind; but as One is never too sure of a Thing we have

have at Heart, fhe liftened to him with a great deal of Attention and Pleafure. As for Mr. *de Canaple*, being folely taken up with feeing her, hearing her, admiring her, he had but little Share in the Converfation.

THE Prefence of Mr. *de Vienne*, whom Mr. *Arundel* had found with the Queen, and who then appeared, took him out of this Happy State, and gave him an Inquietude and Pain, equal to the greateft he had yet felt. This Moment was to decide his Deftiny.

MADAM *de Granfon*, as foon as fhe perceived her Father, went and fell at his Feet, fo full of Fear and Confufion, that it was impoffible for her to bring out a Word; but the Tears which fhe fhed on Mr. *de Vienne*'s Hands, fpoke for her.

I MAKE you no Reproach, my dear Child, faid he, embracing her, the Suc-

cefs

cefs of your Enterprife has juftified it. I only complain of Mr *de Canaple*, who would conceal from me and all Mankind, the Knowledge of an Action fo Generous as his, and who fuffered me to be ignorant of Sentiments which I have more than once wifhed him poffeffed with. Before I durft fpeak to you, Sir, replied Mr. *de Canaple*, it was neceffary to know how fuch Liberty would be taken, and I dare not even now prefume to do it.

And yet I fancy, faid Mr. *de Vienne*, I fhall make no Tyrannical Ufe of my Power, if I lay my Commands on my Daughter to look on You as a Man who fhall very foon be her Hufband. Ah! Sir, cried Mr. *de Canaple*, how fhall I ever be able to thank you as I ought? Will you confent to my Happinefs, Madam? faid he to Madam *de Granfon*, approaching towards her in the moft fubmiffive Manner; fay one Word, only one fingle Word; but confider, my Life depends

upon

upon it. The Step I have taken, said she to him, has said that Word which you ask of me.

MR. *de Canaple*, penetrated with the most lively Joy, expressed it far less by his Speech than by his Transports. Madam *de Granson*, ashamed of so much Love, hastened away to make use of the Permission of going to *Calais*, which Mr. *Arundel* had brought her. Mr. *de Canaple*, Mr. *de Chalons*, and Mr. *de Vienne*, went thither with her. Mr. *de Chalons* waited in a House in the Town for the News which Mr. *de Canaple* was to bring him. Mademoiselle *de Mailly*, successively and almost at the same time a Prey to the greatest Grief and the greatest Joy, wanted but little of Dying with so violent an Agitation. Madam *de Granson* and she embraced each other over and over, and asked, both of them, a thousand Questions at a time. Mademoiselle *de Mailly*, naturally averse to all manner of Dissimulation, emboldened likewise by that solid Virtue

Virtue which she was conscious of to her-self, put no Restraint to her Sentiments. She spoke of Mr. *de Chalons* with all that Tenderness and Acknowledgment which What he had lately done for her, exacted.

WILL you reward him? said the Count *de Canaple* to her; give him Leave to wait on you. It is my Father, replied she, and not my Way of Thinking which is to regulate my Conduct. I hope he will command what I request of you, said the Count *de Canaple*. Mr. *Arundel* has secured the Queen of *England*'s Protection for Mr. *de Chalons*, and Your Marriage is the Price of Mr. *de Mailly*'s Liberty. Ah! said Mademoiselle *de Mailly* again, this Consent must not be extorted from him; Any Happiness would cease to be a Happiness to me, if I obtained it a-gainst his Will.

MR. *de Mailly*, having been prepared by Mr. *de Vienne* for what should be asked of him, heard as he entered his Daughter's Chamber,

Chamber, thefe laft Words; and going to her with open Arms, No, my dear Child, faid he to her, it is not againft my Will you fhall be Happy; I have fuffered, as much as You, the Torments I have put you to. Forget them; it is a Father who loves you, who has always loved you, who afks it of you; and join with me in caufing them to be forgot by Mr. *de Chalons*, whom I will this Moment bring to you. The unhappy State to which Madam *de Mailly* is reduced, no longer allows of any Refentment againft Her, and can give you no Room for any thing but Pity.

MADAM *de Mailly* was really threaten-ed with an approaching Death. The Spleen and Ill-humour which fhe had been a long Time devoured with, and which the ill Succefs of her Artifices likewife redoubled, had caft her into a languifh-ing Diftemper, which grew upon her more and more every Day.

MADAM

MADAM *de Granſon*, to leave Mademoiſelle *de Mailly* the Liberty of receiving Mr. *de Chalons*, went from her; and Mr. *de Mailly*, accompanied by Mr. *de Chalons*, appeared a Moment after; and preſenting him to his Daughter, I ſeparated ye againſt my Will, my dear Children, ſaid he to them, it is with my whole Heart I now rejoin ye.

The Joy of theſe two Perſons, after ſo long an Abſence, after having interchanged ſo many Marks of Tenderneſs, is above Words to expreſs. Mademoiſelle *de Mailly*, warranted by her Father's Preſence, ſaid more endearing Things to Mr. *de Chalons*, than ſhe would have ventured to ſay to him had they been without a Witneſs. For his Part, inebriated with his Happineſs, he made Speeches to her without either Coherence or Conſequence. But after his firſt Tranſports, and when Mr. *de Mailly's* Abſence had left him more at Liberty, he found himſelf enforced to own to her the Suſpicions

cions he had had againſt her.   Tho' they
had produced no other Effect but to make
him unhappy, tho' ſhe might ſtill have
been ignorant of them, he could not be
at Peace with himſelf, till he had aſked
her Pardon for them.

YOU aſk Me Pardon, ſaid ſhe to him!
You to whom I have been the Occaſion
of ſo many different Tortures! You who
was deſirous to give your Life for Me!
You, in ſhort, who loved me at a Time
when you ought to have hated me!

THIS Converſation, ſo full of Charms,
was interrupted by Madam *de Granſon*.
She came to tell Mademoiſelle *de Mailly*,
that the King and Queen of *England*
would the next Day make their Entry
into *Calais*, and that ſhe muſt diſpoſe
herſelf to be preſented to the Queen.

MADAM *de Mailly*'s Death, which happened the ſame Night, inſtead of excuſing
Mademoiſelle *de Mailly* from this Duty,
did on the contrary lay it indiſpenſably
upon her.   It was neceſſary to remove
Mr.

Mr. *de Mailly* from a Place which prefented to him fuch afflicting Objects, and
to obtain Liberty of the Queen for doing
it. I will not grant you this Favour, faid
that Princefs to her when Mademoifelle
de Mailly was prefented to her, but on
Condition that Mr. *de Mailly* will confent
to Your Marriage with Mr. *de Chalons*. I
will have it done at the fame Time with
that of Madam *de Granfon* and Mr. *de Ca-
natle*, before ye fet out from *Calais*.

MY Father's Circumftances and my
own, Madam, replied Mademoifelle *de
Mailly*, enforce us to beg Your Majefty
would pleafe to allow us fome Time for
executing the Orders You vouchfafe to
give us. I ought to refufe your Requeft,
in reward for your making it, replied the
Queen, whom Mr. *Arundel* had before
made acquainted with her Hiftory. Mademoifelle *de Mailly* turn'd her Eyes to
the Ground, blufhing.

THE Queen, after commending her
Modefty, ordered Mr. *de Vienne* to tell

Mr.

4

Mr. *de Mailly* from the King, that He and his Daughter were at Liberty to retire whither they thought fit, provided Mr. *de Chalons* not only received a Renewal of his Promiſe, but likewiſe accompanied them to the Place they ſhould make choice of.

MR. *de Mailly*, who paſſionately wiſhed what was aſked of him, returned the King and Queen his moſt humble Thanks, and ſet out the ſame Day for his Eſtate in *Flanders*, where the Marriage of Mr. *de Chalons* and Mademoiſelle *de Mailly* was celebrated a few Months after.

THAT of Madam *de Granſon* was performed the very next Day, and Mr. *de Canaple* did at laſt enjoy a Happineſs which was given him by the Hands of Love. They went into *Burgundy* to wait for Mr. *de Vienne*, who was obliged to conduct the Inhabitants of *Calais* to King *Philip*.

THESE poor People, forced to forſake their Country, came and begged of him

a new

a new one. Their Fidelity fpoke in their Favour. Lands were given them where they went and fixed their Abode, and where they had no Occafion to lament the Loffes they had fuftained. . *Euftache de Saint-Pierre* and his Family followed the Count *de Canaple*, who gave them a Maintenance fuitable to their Virtue.

THE Queen, finding herfelf with Child, and EDWARD, to ftrengthen his Conqueft, refolving to pafs the Winter at *Calais*, Mr. *Arundel* afked and got Leave for Madam *Arundel* to come thither to him. Mr. *de Mauny* had before, by abundance of Services and Interpofition of Friends, obtained of Mr. *de Liancourt*, both Madam *de Mauny's* Pardon and his own.

F I N I S.